0056804

DATE DUE

MAR. 8 1993	
MAY 1 0 1995	

NK
4399
L9
W3
1985

Watson, Oliver.
Persian lustre ware.

$80.00

PERSIAN LUSTRE WARE

THE FABER MONOGRAPHS ON POTTERY AND PORCELAIN

Present Editors: R.J. CHARLESTON *and* MARGARET MEDLEY

Former Editors: W.B. HONEY, ARTHUR LANE
and SIR HARRY GARNER

BOW PORCELAIN *by* Elizabeth Adams *and* David Redstone
WORCESTER PORCELAIN AND LUND'S BRISTOL *by* Franklin A. Barrett
ROCKINGHAM POTTERY AND PORCELAIN 1745–1842 *by* Alwyn *and* Angela Cox
APOTHECARY JARS *by* Rudolf E.A. Drey
ENGLISH DELFTWARE *by* F.H. Garner *and* Michael Archer
ORIENTAL BLUE AND WHITE *by* Sir Harry Garner
CHINESE CELADON WARES *by* G. St. G.M. Gompertz
SUNG PORCELAIN AND STONEWARE *by* Basil Gray
MASON PORCELAIN AND IRONSTONE *by* Reginald Haggar *and* Elizabeth Adams
LATER CHINESE PORCELAIN *by* Soame Jenyns
JAPANESE POTTERY *by* Soame Jenyns
JAPANESE PORCELAIN *by* Soame Jenyns
ENGLISH PORCELAIN FIGURES OF THE EIGHTEENTH CENTURY *by* Arthur Lane
YÜAN PORCELAIN AND STONEWARE *by* Margaret Medley
T'ANG POTTERY AND PORCELAIN *by* Margaret Medley
ENGLISH BROWN STONEWARE *by* Adrian Oswald, R.J.C. Hildyard *and* R.G. Hughes
CREAMWARE *by* Donald Towner
ENGLISH BLUE AND WHITE PORCELAIN OF THE EIGHTEENTH CENTURY
by Bernard Watney
PERSIAN LUSTRE WARE *by* Oliver Watson
ENGLISH TRANSFER-PRINTED POTTERY AND PORCELAIN *by* Cyril Williams-Wood

PERSIAN LUSTRE WARE

OLIVER WATSON

faber and faber

LONDON · BOSTON

First published in 1985
by Faber and Faber Limited
3 Queen Square, London WC1

Filmset and printed in Great Britain by
Jolly & Barber Ltd, Rugby, Warwickshire

Extract from *The Koran Interpreted* translated by
Arthur J. Arberry, reprinted with permission of
George Allen & Unwin (Publishers) Ltd and
Macmillan Publishing Company:
© George Allen & Unwin Ltd, 1955

British Library Cataloguing in Publication Data

Watson, Oliver
Persian lustre ware. — (Faber monographs on pottery and porcelain)
1. Lustre-ware — Iran — History
2. Lustre-ware, Islamic — Iran — History
I. Title
738.3′0955   NK4399.L9
ISBN 0-571-13235-9

Library of Congress Cataloguing in Publication Data has been applied for

FOREWORD

Of all the techniques by which pottery has been decorated throughout its history, lustre-painting has in its day perhaps awakened the most intense blend of curiosity and admiration. Its variety of colour and play of iridescence, often patently affected by the chances of the kiln, have made it one of the most unpredictable and seductive of ornamental devices. To the mid-nineteenth century, with its romantic susceptibility to things oriental, it seemed infinitely fascinating, not least because by then the technical knowledge of how to make it seemed to have been lost from the world, although the Staffordshire potters of the early nineteenth century had used it in their own prosaic way, mainly in fields of plain colour. The challenge to 'rediscover' it was taken up by such artist-potters as William de Morgan in England and Clément Massier in France, where the term *poterie à reflets métalliques* seems to have added a special allure. The history of the technique, however, for long known mainly from the Hispano-Moresque pottery of Spain, and to a lesser extent from the lustred maiolica of Deruta and Gubbio in Italy, was obscure. It had certainly been used in Safavid Persia, and from the last years of the nineteenth century the increasing pace of archaeology in the Near East brought to light lustred wares which were obviously earlier—but how much earlier? Examples came to light in Egypt, Syria, Mesopotamia and, above all, Persia. But how did all these different wares relate to each other, and how were they to be dated? This puzzle has been almost a century in the unravelling, and certainly the whole story is still not told. Equally certainly, however, the role of Iran in this history is of key importance, and it is on lustre-pottery in Iran—and particularly in Kashan—that Dr Oliver Watson, the author of the present book, has concentrated his attention. Starting as an academic dissertation, the work has been adapted and expanded to tell a more general story. Its appearance not only brings new precision into a hitherto somewhat confused field, but presents the reader with a particularly successful piece of ceramic detection.

R.J. CHARLESTON

CONTENTS

PREFACE

This book grew from a Ph.D. thesis completed in 1977 at the School of Oriental and African Studies, University of London, under the supervision of Dr Géza Fehérvári. To him especially my thanks are due, as they are to all those who helped me both in that research and in the task of turning it into a book. Curators, archaeologists, collectors, dealers and fellow students have all been very generous with time, information and photographs. I must record a particular debt of gratitude to Raymond Ades and his family, whose collection of 'Gurgan' ware is unequalled: they have allowed me generous access to it, and, not least, have permitted me to publish pieces from it as 'Kashan' ware. I am grateful to Alan Caiger-Smith for technical information on the lustre technique and for his comments on Chapter 3, and to Manijeh Bayani for help with the poem on page 80. My thanks are also due to Jane Arrowsmith, who typed the greater part of a difficult manuscript, and to family, friends and colleagues who have suggested many improvements in style and content. The collecting of data is a never-ending task; I should be most grateful to hear of new information, particularly about signed or dated pieces, that would add to, emend or refute the hypotheses presented here.

OLIVER WATSON
Department of Ceramics
Victoria and Albert Museum
London

ILLUSTRATIONS

COLOUR PLATES
between pages 130 and 131

MONOCHROME PLATES

ILLUSTRATIONS

LINE DRAWINGS

MAP

PHOTOGRAPHIC ACKNOWLEDGMENTS

I owe a debt of thanks to many individuals and institutions without whose help I could not have obtained the wide range of illustrations I had wanted. I am particularly grateful to Brian Morgan of Bluetts for his photographs of the Ades Family Collection, to Edmund de Unger for photographs from the Keir Collection and to Nasser Khalili for photographs from his own collection. Sheikh Nasser and Sheikha Hussa al-Sabah have generously allowed me to reproduce a number of pieces from their collections. Colleagues in other museums have greatly aided me, in particular Michael Rogers from the British Museum, Marilyn Jenkins from the Metropolitan Museum of Art, Marthe Bernus from the Louvre, Esin Atil from the Freer Gallery of Art, James Allan from the Ashmolean Museum, André Leth from the David Collection, Ellen Smart from the Walters Art Gallery, Robin Crighton from the Fitzwilliam Museum and Ekkart Klinge from the Hetjens Museum. Messrs Sotheby's have generously provided photographs of pieces from their sales. Dr Chahriyar Adle helped with photographs from the Musée de Sèvres and Dr Yusuf Kiani with photographs from the Iran Bastan Museum. To these people and to other institutions who provided photographs go my thanks. The photographs of objects in the British Museum and those from the Victoria and Albert Museum are reproduced by courtesy of their respective Trustees.

NOTES ON DATING

The Islamic era began with the Prophet's *Hijra* or Migration from Mecca to Medina on 16 July AD 622. The Islamic year is lunar, made up of six thirty-day and six twenty-nine-day months, and is eleven days shorter than the Christian year. There is thus no fixed correspondence between the Islamic and Christian calendars, the Islamic year beginning eleven days earlier in each Christian year. Precise equivalents can be found with the help of such concordances as G.S.P. Freeman-Grenville, *The Muslim and Christian Calendars* (London, 1977). Each Islamic year or month is likely to overlap two Christian years or months. Thus the Islamic year 600 (*Hijri* or H) ran from 10 September 1203 AD to 28 August 1204 and its first month, Muharram, from 10 September to 10 October. To avoid overloading the text, and making comparisons cumbersome and confusing, it is proposed here to give only the Christian year or year and month in which the Islamic equivalent started: e.g. 600/1203, or Muharram 600/September 1203. Only Christian centuries are used, though to within a few years the twelfth century AD corresponds to the sixth century H, the thirteenth AD to the seventh H and the fourteenth AD to the eighth H.

The Islamic months are:

1	Muharram	5	Jumada I	9	Ramadan
2	Safar	6	Jumada II	10	Shawwal
3	Rabi' I	7	Rajab	11	Dhu'l-Qa'da
4	Rabi' II	8	Sha'ban	12	Dhu'l-Hijja

CASPIAN SEA

Baku

■ TABRIZ

• Takht-i-
Sulaiman

GURGA
■

TEHRAN
■ RAYY
• Veramin

• Damgha

Samarra

Sava •

Sultanabad •

■ QUMM

• Aran

■ KASHAN

Quhrud •

• Natanz

■ BAGHDAD

Tigris

Najaf

Euphrates

ISFAHAN ■

Linjan

• Kuhpaya

■ YAZD

SHIRAZ ■

Kharg•

Sarvistan•

• Shahr-i Ij

Siraf
•

• Khonj

PERSIAN GULF

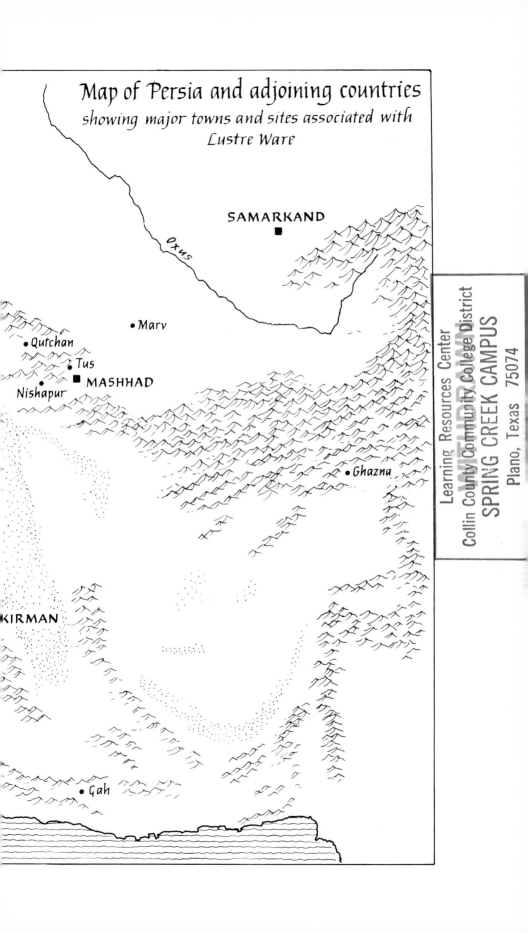

Map of Persia and adjoining countries
showing major towns and sites associated with
Lustre Ware

SAMARKAND

Oxus

• Marv

• Qutchan

• Tus

■ MASHHAD

Nishapur

• Ghazna

KIRMAN

• Gah

Chapter 1

INTRODUCTION

Persian lustre pottery has attracted a large bibliography over the last century for three principal reasons. It is a luxury ware, often with painted decoration of great sophistication; it can be found in Western museums in large quantities, and the inscriptions frequently contain dates or potters' signatures. The combination of high quality, accessibility and a large amount of documentary evidence is difficult for scholars to resist. The justification for the present study is that it is based on a far greater quantity of documentary material than previous studies—on published information gathered from diverse sources and a significant amount of new material.

This book deals with the lustre technique alone, and not with other closely related decorative techniques, although these are referred to in places. The reason is that we can give a far more detailed account of lustre ware than we can of any other. The quality of painting makes possible precise stylistic divisions, while dates and signatures produce chronological and workshop distinctions. The identification of buildings for which tiles were made means that we can consider them in their intended context. This contrasts greatly even with the most complex contemporary wares, some at least of which were made by the same potters in the same workshops—e.g. *minai* enamelled or underglaze-painted pottery. For these we can do no more at present than produce rough stylistic groupings, and indicate the few dated and fewer signed pieces.

Vessels and tiles from the late twelfth to the mid-fourteenth century form the greater part of the material. These divide into two groups: the 'pre-Mongol' wares, which date from the half century or so preceding the devastating impact of the Mongol invasion of central Persia in 1220; and the 'Il-Khanid' wares, which are named after the Mongol dynasty that established itself in Persia from the mid-thirteenth century onwards. The wares of later centuries are included to complete the history of the technique, although they survive in smaller numbers and with less supporting documentary evidence.

The technical complexity of lustre ware gives it a further special interest, for we are forced to see its production over the centuries as a single, continuous tradition—the precise formulation of pigment and unique firing procedure taught by master to apprentice for generations. The dismal efforts of the modern potter belong to a technical tradition that stretches back directly and unbroken to the masterpieces of the thirteenth century.

What is attempted in this book is solely a study of ceramic history. However, points of wider interest are touched upon that are worthy of much deeper consideration than is possible here. One such question, briefly discussed in Chapter 11, is the meaning of images and inscriptions on tiles. Further elucidation is highly desirable, for this is the first time that these images and inscriptions can be seen in the precise social context for which they were made—in this case the funerary monuments of a minority sect. Further research will perhaps offer us more than the vague speculation which has characterized so much of the study of Islamic 'iconography' to date.

The consideration of lustre ware production in relation to political history also raises interesting questions. In the past, the term 'Saljuq' has often been applied by art historians to those wares here called 'pre-Mongol', following a convention which attaches the name of the ruling political dynasty to artifacts produced within its lands. This suggests that the wealthy communities on which the production of luxury goods depends are created by stable and centralized political power. While this may generally hold true, it is evidently not the case in the 'pre-Mongol' period. The Turkish Saljuqs had taken control of Persia in the mid-eleventh century, and ruled an empire that stretched from Balkh in the east to Baghdad in the west. By the 1170s, however, when the first lustre pots were made, this empire had collapsed into a patchwork of small states engaged in almost constant warfare. To describe this period as 'Saljuq' is inaccurate and misleading. Moreover, the political conditions seem most inauspicious for the development of luxury goods. Yet we find, in metalwork as much as in ceramics, a marked increase in output accompanied by an extraordinary fecundity of new technical and decorative ideas. This unparalleled artistic boom at a time of apparent political turmoil is a phenomenon as yet unexplained.

The repetitive nature of designs and inscriptions, and the virtual absence of dedications to individuals indicate that the pottery was not, with rare exceptions (see pages 52 and 108), made to special order for high-ranking patrons, but was a commercial product dependent on a 'middle-class' market. The economy of the country as a whole was flourishing sufficiently to provide markets for these luxury goods. The political situation cannot have been so troubled as to prevent merchants travelling the length and breadth of the country to satisfy their customers—a fact made plain by the occurrence of lustre sherds at virtually every archaeological site in Persia.

The Mongol invasions disrupted one of the most remarkable periods of ceramic innovation the world has ever seen. Provoked initially by the ill-judged execution of Mongol envoys and merchants by a provincial governor, the Mongols swept across the country, destroying towns, massacring populations and burning crops. The impact on commercial life can be seen immediately from the dated lustre pieces: a high level of production was maintained until 1219, but from the next forty years only four dated vessels and a handful of tiles survive.

The prolific 'Il-Khanid' production, which was a resumption of work by the pre-Mongol ateliers after this hiatus, came virtually to a halt in 1340. We are forced to note the coincidence of the fragmentation of the Il-Khanid state at the same time. A few pieces bridge the gap between then and the seventeenth-century Safavid wares and show that the technical tradition was maintained. They are of poor quality and even those with the name of Abu Sa'id, the Timurid Sultan, have a distinctly provincial aspect. The revived fashion for lustre wares in the seventeenth century, when Persia was ruled by the Safavid dynasty, seems almost an afterthought in the general revival of ceramic arts in that period, coming well after the great development of blue-and-white wares. The declining production of this particular group may have accompanied the decline in the country's fortunes in the eighteenth century and the disruptions of the Afghan invasions. The last revival of the technique in the late nineteenth century under the Qajars may in large part have been caused by the interest then being shown by Europeans in Persian antiquities, and in lustre ware in particular.

Chapter 2

THE CERAMIC BACKGROUND

Neither the lustre technique, nor the type of ceramic vessel to which it was applied, were Persian innovations, though the Persian potters brought both to a new level of artistic and technical perfection. A new ceramic body, the so-called 'frit' ware, had revolutionized Persian ceramics before the arrival of the lustre technique. It may therefore be clearer if we review the earlier history of both lustre and frit ware separately, before considering Persian lustred ceramics as an entity.

In the centuries before the advent of frit ware, Persian potters made use of common earthenware clays. These were generally of red or buff colour, often with an overcoat of white slip to provide a suitable ground for various decorative techniques. They were covered by a thin transparent lead glaze that could, when required, be stained green or amber by the addition of copper or iron oxides respectively. Some techniques were widespread throughout the country—colour splashing and simple sgraffito decoration, for example—while others were restricted to certain districts. Slip painting predominated in the east, while in the north and north-west various styles of *champlevé* and sgraffito decoration were characteristic.[1] These wares were in general crudely fashioned, and impress us now rather by the vigour than the sophistication of their designs; Arthur Lane's description of them as the 'Ceramic Underworld' perhaps rates them too low. The one exception to these generalizations—the epigraphic Samanid ware from Nishapur and Samarkand—shows a more careful finish to the pot, and some of the finest calligraphy surviving from the period. Even these wares, sophisticated as they are, nevertheless appear to be largely for local consumption. While some wares may have been exported to Nishapur from Samarkand, though this is not yet altogether clear, eastern slip-

[1]The best general introduction, though now outdated in certain aspects is Lane (1947); see also Fehérvári (1973). Pope (1939) is so unreliable as to be virtually worthless as a history of ceramics in Persia, but is useful as a source of illustrations. A full bibliography is found in Grube (1976).

painted wares have not been found on any western Persian site,[2] and the north and north-western slip wares again appear highly localized. The general status of these pots was low, rising above that of kitchen ware but, with few exceptions, was not in any way comparable with contemporary luxury products, such as vessels in silver or bronze, or the finer works of the glass-maker.

The use of the frit rather than the clay body allowed the potter to improve considerably the technical finish of his product. The frit body—a mixture of ground quartz with small amounts of white clay and glaze (see page 32 for a detailed description)—is first seen in Egypt in the twelfth or perhaps as early as the eleventh century.[3] It is a material adapted from the ancient 'Egyptian faience', making use of a technique that may have survived since pre-Islamic times in the manufacture of beads and other small trinkets. We must presume that the technique came from Egypt to Persia at some point in the first half of the twelfth century, but exactly when and in what way we do not know. It appears that it was only the material that was adopted in Persia, for among the early Persian frit wares we see no examples of Egyptian shapes or designs.[4]

The Persian potter seems originally to have taken the material for a single purpose—to copy the fine white Chinese Sung porcelains then being imported into the Middle East in large quantities. These porcelains differed from earlier imports in the fineness of their walls, which left them translucent, and their delicate incised or moulded decoration. These could not be imitated, as the earlier heavy porcelain bowls had been, by the use of a thick, opaque-white, glaze. The frit body could provide the counterfeit: it was pure white under its colourless transparent glaze, it could be thrown and turned finely, and when thin was in fact translucent. The earliest Persian products in this material are close copies of Chinese originals, but within a short period of time the Persian taste for colour and design had made itself felt.[5] Glazes were stained blue, turquoise, green or purple; carved patterns of purely Islamic origin appeared. A new range of vessel shapes was made, some based on the earlier clay-bodied vessels, others derived from metal forms; and new decorative techniques were invented.

By the year 1200, a range of techniques was in use that was only surpassed by the industrial potters of eighteenth-century England. Sgraffito, carved, pierced and openwork decoration; the use of moulds and applied decoration; underglaze- and enamel-painting, gilding and lustre-painting; all these

[2]The single sherd found in the excavations at Rayy and now in the University Museum, Philadelphia, highlights rather than contradicts their absence in the West.
[3]Helen Philon, *Early Islamic Ceramics*, Benaki Museum, Athens, 1980, pp. 176–7.
[4]The absence of prototypes in Persia argues that the technique is a foreign invention introduced at a particular moment. The Egyptian wares show a wide spectrum of body types from clay to frit. See Allan (1974), and Philon (1980).
[5]See A. Lane, 'Sung Wares and the Seljuq Pottery of Persia', *Transactions of The Oriental Ceramic Society*, XXII, 1946–7.

characterized one of the most creative periods of ceramic development seen anywhere in the world. By the end of the twelfth century many towns in Persia were producing the simpler types of frit wares—wasters and other evidence have been found at Nishapur, Gurgan, Rayy and Kashan, and the wide variety of types and quality suggests an even larger number of centres.[6] The more sophisticated techniques, in particular lustre- and enamel-painting, appear to have been restricted to a single centre (see page 37ff). We are hampered, however, in the precise dating of much of this ware by the fact that dates only appear on the lustre-, enamel- and underglaze-painted wares. These techniques all appear to have been developed after the initial period of experimentation that followed the introduction of the frit body—they do not appear on shapes closely related to the Chinese, nor on the hard, dense frit bodies with which these shapes are associated. The earliest date—on a lustre piece of 1179 (Plate 37)—is probably a number of decades into the frit-ware period, but we have no strong reason to suppose that this date does not mark, within a few years, the introduction of lustre painting into Persia. Similarly, the earliest dates for enamel painting (1186) and for underglaze painting (1204) probably mark in rough terms the invention of these techniques. The latter two techniques are rightly termed inventions, for they are nowhere to be found, even in China, at an earlier date than this. The same is not true for lustre, which had already a long history in the Islamic world.

THE EARLIER HISTORY OF LUSTRE

The technical complexities of lustre painting, described in detail in the following chapter, are such that one may reasonably assume that no medieval potter, however resourceful or inventive, could have independently discovered its secrets. Unlike every other decorative technique, the lustre pot gives no clue in the finished article as to the manner of its making. We must therefore assume that the process was from its very inception maintained as a continuous tradition, the knowledge of the technique being passed on from generation to generation. If that knowledge had been lost it would not have been regained.

This assumption is the basis of the 'migration theory' of lustre pottery: that the history of the rise and decline of lustre production in the various countries of the Middle East is explained by the movement of potters taking their 'secret' with them, and not by the imitation of imported articles by local potters. Lustre is by its nature an expensive product. It requires expensive materials, and a second firing (which alone, involving extra fuel and labour, may have as much as doubled its price). The potting and the painting are usually of a high

[6]C. K. Wilkinson, *Nishapur*, New York, 1973, pp. 260–1; Pope (1937); sherds and other material from Rayy are held in the University Museum, Philadelphia and the Museum of Fine Arts, Boston; and from Gurgan in the Iran Bastan Museum in Tehran.

order. The high cost of the ware, and the resulting profit to the potter must have been a considerable inducement to those who held the secret to keep it as a monopoly. There is considerable evidence in Persia, as elsewhere in the Middle East and indeed in Europe, that such a monopoly was preserved. The technical sophistication of lustre and the resulting possibility of monopoly go a long way towards explaining the uniform nature of a country's lustre ware at any one time, and the apparent suddenness with which production stopped at one place, and started at another.[7]

Much energy has been expended by scholars in the past on crediting one country rather than another with the invention of the lustre technique.[8] Precise facts about its early use are exceedingly scarce, and do not provide sufficient information to construct a secure history. Preliminary results from excavations, notably those from Siraf on the Persian Gulf, suggest that the conventional 'accepted view' may have the dates of some types wrong by as much as a century.[9] In the absence of any detailed or reliable study, however, the 'accepted view' is here offered with due warning.

The earliest datable lustre decoration occurs on a glass goblet found at Fostat (the old city of Cairo) bearing the name of a certain Abd al-Samad ibn Ali, who governed Egypt for one month in 773. Another fragment bears the date 779 in Coptic numerals, and both are thought to be of Egyptian origin.[10] It has been suggested that the technique developed out of certain types of late Roman enamelled glass, which used silver as a stain in a similar way to the lustre technique.[11] The next identifiable occurrence is in Mesopotamia, both on glass and also, for the first time, on pottery. It is possible that the Egyptian craftsmen were attracted by the wealth of the country where the Abbasid caliphs held court. Many fragments of lustred pottery were found in the palace city of Samarra, situated above Baghdad on the Tigris, and occupied by the caliphs between 838 and 883. Based on this dating, and that of a group of lustred tiles apparently sent from Baghdad to Kairouan, in Tunisia, in 862, Kühnel posited a chronology for the Mesopotamian lustre wares.[12] He took those pieces with polychrome decoration to be the earliest, with a change to a bichrome palette taking place about 860. By about 880 a monochrome palette was adopted. Pieces painted in a monochrome lustre with curiously stylized animals and humans are generally attributed to the tenth century. At some point in this century production of lustred pottery ceases in Mesopotamia, and starts in Egypt (the second migration) under the Fatimids. Thus far the story is based

[7]Watson (1975b, pp. 65–6).
[8]See the bibliography in Grube (1976, p. 342).
[9]D. Whitehouse, 'Islamic Glazed Pottery in Iraq and the Persian Gulf: The Ninth and Tenth Centuries', *Annali dell'Istituto Orientale di Napoli*, 39, 1979, pp. 15–16.
[10]London (1976, no. 119).
[11]C. J. Lamm, *Oriental Glass*, Stockholm, 1941, p. 20ff.
[12]E. Kühnel, 'Die Abbasidischen Lüsterfayencen', *Ars Islamica*, I, 1934.

on a mass of material but little secure data. The accuracy and relevance of both the Samarra and Kairouan dating have been questioned, and the Siraf results may change our view drastically. The question of early lustre production outside Mesopotamia, particularly in Egypt, has been raised.[13]

When dealing with the Fatimid production in Egypt we are on firmer ground. Provenance is securely established by the thousands of sherds found in Fostat, and by inscriptions on a number of them. A number of signatures which occur frequently allow a rough grouping of types. It is greatly to be regretted that a study to produce a detailed chronology has not yet been undertaken.[14] The earliest datable pieces bear dedications which can be ascribed to about the year 1000. Production seems to stop suddenly at some point in the second half of the twelfth century, for no lustres are found with typically Ayyubid styles of decoration. It is frequently pointed out that the take-over of Egypt by Saladin and the establishment of the Ayyubids in 1171, precede by only a very few years the earliest Persian lustre piece of 1179 (Plate 37). The change of dynasty may have been a less immediate cause of the third migration than the burning of the suburb of Fostat in 1168, and, more generally, the social unrest, famine and economic hardship that accompanied the last years of Fatimid rule. However, at some point in the second half of the twelfth century lustre production ceases in Egypt and starts in Syria (with the so-called 'Tel Minis' and 'Raqqa' wares)[15] and in Persia.

We had better deal here with the argument, put forward most strongly by A. U. Pope in the *Survey of Persian Art*, that lustre was made in Persia before the end of the twelfth century. Two arguments are put forward. First, a large number of tenth-century lustre pieces including wasters are said to have been found in Persia, and secondly a frieze of lustre tiles in the shrine at Mashhad bears the date 1118.[16] The tenth-century lustres from Persia cannot, however, be distinguished in style of decoration, glaze, body material or vessel shape from those accepted as being Mesopotamian. Mesopotamian lustres, with their consistent types of decoration, glaze and clay, have been found in small quantities on sites at both ends of the Islamic empire—at Brahminabad in Sind and at Medinat al-Zahra in Spain[17] and on virtually every major site between them. Large quantities are found exported to Egypt, and there is no reason to suppose that numbers were not also exported to Persia. The excavators at Rayy and Nishapur—both major conurbations in the relevant period—found, however, so few sherds of lustre that they deemed them all to

[13]R. Schnyder, 'Tulunidische Lüsterfayencen', *Ars Orientalis*, V, 1963.
[14]An attempt at a rough chronology is given by H. Philon, op. cit. (above, note 3), which is the most detailed study to date.
[15]V. Porter, *Medieval Syrian Pottery*, Ashmolean Museum, Oxford, 1981, pp. 3–8, and V. Porter and O. Watson, 'Tell Minis Wares' (forthcoming).
[16]Pope (1939, pp. 1493, 1626 and 1548).
[17]Hobson (1932, pp. 8–9); A. W. Frothingham, *Lustreware of Spain*, New York, 1951, pp. 4–6.

1   BOWL. Egyptian, 12th century, diameter 29.6 cm (11.6 in)
    Keir Collection. See page 28

2   BOWL. Monumental style, diameter 15.5 cm (6.1 in)
    National Museum, Damascus, A14294. See page 28

be imports.[18] The 'wasters' claimed by Pope, found at Sava, were disputed as being such by Ettinghausen[19] and were never illustrated or fully described. It would seem prudent to disregard claims of a tenth-century production in Persia until more substantial arguments can be produced.

The frieze of tiles at Mashhad must be taken more seriously. It is found on the walls of the shrine's tomb-chamber, and is set between a large Quranic inscription frieze and panels of dado stars which it surmounts (Plate 105). The tiles measure about 10 cm (4 in) high, less than a quarter of the height of the Quranic inscription. The inscription is set in contour panels filled with a peacock-eye motif. The tiles have been reset and are in a very jumbled order, with several serious lacunae. The text records restorations done in the tombs and a series of names, including that of the Saljuq sultan Sanjar, a queen Turkan Zumurrud, and a person by the name of al-Hasan ibn Muhammad.[20] The date 1118 is quite clear, while the Quranic frieze and star and octagonal tiles below are dated 1215 (see page 124). There are several compelling reasons for thinking that the tiles of 1118 are not of the date inscribed on them, but are a replacement of an original text, possibly in brick, destroyed during the renovations of 1215. Their insignificant size suggests this, while the same style of inscription is found on a star tile in the dado. This star bears a name which also occurs on the mihrab in the same shrine also dated 1215. The large dishes with contour panels with which Pope associated the style of the frieze of 1118 are not of the early twelfth century, but can be dated to about the year 1200 (page 86, Colour Plate D, Plate 58).[21]

We cannot deny that early lustres have been found in Persia, but can find no strong reason to assume they were made there. The Mashhad frieze and the associated dishes are of the early thirteenth century, and no other material offers itself as evidence of a continuous Persian production from the tenth century onwards.

The lustre of the late twelfth century in Persia starts suddenly and can be best explained by the arrival of Egyptian craftsmen. The close similarities of certain Egyptian and Persian pieces strongly suggest such a connection. Compare for a moment the pieces illustrated in Plates 1 and 2. Plate 1 shows a fine, typical piece of Egyptian lustre. The naturalistic drawing of the mythical animal is painted in reserve against a lustre ground. Foliate sprays issue from its mouth, wings and tail, and float between the feet, to break up the uniform area of lustre. Round the walls runs an undulating stem from which sprouts on alternate sides split-palmette foliage. The Persian 'monumental style' bowl shown in Plate 2 is made up of precisely the same elements: a central animal reserved on a lustre ground that is broken up with foliate sprays, and an

[18]Wilkinson, op. cit., pp. 181–2; E. F. Schmidt (1936, p. 83).
[19]A. U. Pope, 'The *Survey of Persian Art* and its Critics', *Ars Islamica*, IX, 1942, p. 184, note 17.
[20]See Combe (1913, no. 2978) and P. Sykes, 'Historical Notes on Khurasan', *Journal of the Royal Asiatic Society*, 1910, pp. 1140–1.
[21]This argument is given fully in Watson (1977, pp. 35–7).

3   DISH. Egyptian, 12th century, diameter 38.3 cm (15.1 in)
     Courtesy of the Freer Gallery of Art, Smithsonian Institution, Washington D.C., 41.12.
     See page 30

4   DISH. Monumental style, diameter 35.5 cm (14 in)
     The Cleveland Museum of Art, purchase from the J.H. Wade Fund, 44.74. See pages 30,
     48 and 52

undulating stem with split-palmette foliage round the walls. The formal similarity of these two pieces is very striking, but in many pieces less obviously comparable elements held in common by both, indicate a close connection. For example, the horsemen in Plates 3 and 4 share the same half-moon border and guard-stripe, and essentially the same pose of both horse and rider. Similar inscriptions also appear on both Egyptian and Persian wares (see pages 52 and 71). A number of changes have of course been made in the Persian pieces – the use of a particularly Persian form of the half-palmette and the adoption of the large, round face with fine features that typifies the ideal of Persian beauty.

The similarities of style and motif, together with the coincidence in date of the end of lustre production in Egypt and its beginning in Persia, are strong enough arguments in themselves to indicate some kind of movement of potters. An understanding of the technical complexities of lustre leads us to expect no less.

Chapter 3

TECHNIQUE

Lustre is an over-glaze technique, in that the pigment is applied in a second firing at a lower temperature than the first, and is applied to the surface of a hard, fired glaze. However, unlike enamel pigments, lustre is imperceptible to the touch, being of the order of one micron in thickness.

A simplified description of the pigment and its firing is as follows: the pigment itself consists of a mixture of compounds of silver and copper finely ground together with a refractory earthy medium, which is painted on to the surface of an already fired glaze. The piece is fired to a temperature at which the glaze softens slightly, but not to the extent that the earthy medium will adhere. During this firing, or during a certain part of it, the supply of air to the fire is restricted to give a reducing atmosphere by the production of carbon monoxide. This unstable gas will extract oxygen from any available source, and the silver and copper compounds, converted to oxides during the heating, give up their oxygen and are deposited as a thin metallic layer bonded into the glaze. When the firing is complete, the medium is removed by polishing, and the layer of lustre revealed: the lustre's thinness gives the multi-coloured and mother-of-pearl reflections for which it is valued (see Colour Plate O). The colour of the lustre depends upon a number of factors, in particular the relative quantities of copper and silver, the composition of the glaze and the firing temperature. Silver usually gives a yellowish tone, copper a red one.[1]

We are very fortunate that there survives a description of pottery making which was written in 700/1300 by a certain Abu'l-Qasim, brother of Yusuf of the Abu'l-Tahir family which dominated lustre pottery production in Kashan for at least four generations (see page 178). Yusuf and Abu'l-Qasim belong to the last recorded generation; Abu'l-Qasim, perhaps a younger brother, did not

---

[1]Caiger-Smith (1973, pp. 25–7), Watson (1975b). Alan Caiger-Smith, himself a practising potter in the lustre technique, discusses the technique more fully in his book *Lustre Pottery*, see Caiger-Smith (1985).

become a potter but ended up as a court historian at the Mongol capital in Tabriz, where amongst other works he contributed to the monumental *Jami' al-Tawarikh* or 'Compilation of Histories' under the direction of the great Mongol vizier, Rashid al-Din. At the end of a work on precious stones, perfumes and other substances he added an appendix on the art of pottery, which he described as a 'kind of alchemy'. This text gives detailed information on the substances required, their geographical sources, the proportions in which they should be combined, as well as a practical description of the methods of manufacture and decoration. An excellent translation and commentary has been published by Dr James Allan, and this has been used as the basis for the following account.[2]

The body of both vessels and tiles is formed from a quartz frit. This consists of ten parts of finely ground and sifted quartz (found as pebbles in river beds), mixed with one part of sticky white clay, to give the mixture some degree of plasticity, and one part of glaze mixture, which acts to bond the quartz particles together. The fineness of the paste varies, depending on the size of article to be made. Larger particles allow a thick slab of clay to dry more evenly throughout its fabric by allowing air to pass more easily through it, thus preventing warping and cracking caused by differential shrinkage. Small articles can have a finer and denser paste.

The glaze is formed of a roughly equal mixture of ground quartz and the ashes of a desert plant which contain a very high proportion of alkaline salts. These act as a flux and cause the quartz to vitrify at a manageable temperature. The two alone will produce a transparent glaze. They are heated together, and when molten poured into water, which shatters the glass thus formed. These fragments are further ground and suspended in water before application. An opaque white glaze is formed by the addition to this mixture of a small amount of tin oxide, which has been made by roasting tin together with lead. The glaze may also be coloured by the addition of copper oxides, which gives a turquoise colour, or cobalt, which gives a dark blue. In fine quality wares the turquoise glaze is normally also made opaque by the addition of the tin oxide, whereas the cobalt blue is almost invariably transparent. The two coloured glazes and the white tin glaze are occasionally combined in radial panels (Plates 22 and 23).

Abu'l-Qasim describes the forming of the vessels thus: 'This [the paste] is kneaded well like dough and left to mature for one night. In the morning it is well beaten by hand and the mastercraftsman makes it into fine vessels on the potter's wheel; these are left standing until they are half dry. They are scraped down on the wheel and the feet are added, and when they are dry they are washed with a damp linen cloth in order to smooth over the lines on them so

---

[2]The Persian text, including a facsimile of the original manuscript, is published by Afshar (1967). Allan (1973) relies for his translation on the edition by H. Ritter et al. (1935). Quotations cited here are taken from Allan's translation. Technical studies relevant to wares of this period are found in Allan (1974) and Dayton (1977).

that they disappear. When they are dry again they are rubbed with a wool cloth until they are clean and smooth.'[3]

This description is very revealing, in particular in the turning and finishing of the pot when in a dry or semi-dry state. This alone can account for the extremely thin walls of many of the vessels, which would have been impossible to throw directly on the wheel; the very fine and subtle profiles of many of the pieces can also only have been achieved in this way. Abu'l-Qasim does not mention the use of moulds, though the surviving objects show how extensive was this method of manufacture (e.g. Plates 24, 31, 33–6). Moulds were used for both dishes and closed forms, and in the manufacture of tiles. The process of forming tiles with relief inscriptions must have been fairly complicated. It would appear that a single mould was used to form the body of the tile, together with those parts, such as decorative cornices, which were repeated from tile to tile. The letters of the inscription were then formed separately, taken from a design presumably worked out on paper, and luted on to the tile surface. A very few moulds for bowls, or masters from which moulds were taken, are known, all made from unglazed fired clay.[4]

Once the finished article was dry, it was ready for glazing. There is no reason to assume, as Dr Allan does, that there was a biscuit firing, for Abu'l-Qasim mentions none, and indeed he calls the enamelled ware 'wares of two fires', which implies that the glaze firing must be the first.[5] The glaze is applied in liquid form, and the excess left to drip off before the piece is dried in the sun.

It is at this point that colours other than lustre are applied, for in general the lustre wares under discussion have an opaque white glaze, and the colours were not painted directly on to the body as in underglaze-painted wares. Copper oxides for turquoise, and cobalt oxides for blue are the only colourings used and are painted with a little water directly on to the dry powdery surface of the raw glaze, as in the European maiolica or delftware technique. The turquoise colour is volatile and tends to blur, while the powerful action of cobalt as a flux occasionally causes whole areas of glaze to flow, particularly on the tiles, where it is used in great quantities. The turquoise is mostly used to colour small areas, such as garments or flower-heads, where its area may be defined more sharply by the lustre pigment applied later. The cobalt, when not applied too heavily, retains its definition and it is used to outline panels and cartouches, for quite precise details of design and, on the tiles, to colour the raised inscriptions.

The first firing, thought to be at a little under 1000° C, lasts about a week, according to Abu'l-Qasim, including the period of cooling. This implies a kiln of no mean size. Abu'l-Qasim also states that the vessels are protected each in

---

[3]Allan (1973, para. 23).

[4]No moulds for lustre wares have been found, but see the moulds for frit wares found in excavations at Nishapur in Wilkinson, *Nishapur*, New York, 1973, pp. 272–5, nos. 57–68.

[5]Allan is partly led to his conclusion by a minor error in the editing of the Persian text he used, see Watson (1977, p. 31, note 5).

its own saggar, placed on long pegs of clay set into the kiln walls. Remains of such pegs and kiln walls with rows of holes into which they fit have been found in various parts of Iran, and this must have been a standard procedure.[6]

The vessels or tiles emerge from the first firing covered in the hard white glaze, with colour in the appropriate places, and are ready for the lustre painting. In addition to the metallic compounds already mentioned, the pigment contains small amounts of iron and sulphur compounds, which help the reduction, and it is diluted with grape juice or vinegar.[7] The glaze, being hard, allows designs to be scratched through the thin lustre pigment on to it. The second firing takes place, Abu'l-Qasim tells us, in a special kiln '. . . specially made for this purpose', where the pieces are subject to '. . . light smoke for seventy-two hours until they acquire the colour of two firings. When they are cold, take them out and rub them with damp earth so that the colour of gold comes out. . . . That which has been evenly fired reflects like red gold and shines like the light of the sun.'[8]

From Piccolpasso's descriptions of lustre ware in mid-sixteenth-century Italy, and from the experiences of Alan Caiger-Smith, a studio potter who has for some twenty years been producing lustre wares in Aldermaston, Berkshire, it is apparent that Abu'l-Qasim has fastened upon the essentials of the lustre technique. Quite apart from the make-up of the pigment, the kiln design is of crucial importance. Piccolpasso reports the Italian potters' view that the whole art of lustre pottery lay in the method of making the kiln, to the extent that they were kept in locked rooms. For on the kiln design depended the control over temperature and atmosphere upon which the success of the technique rested.[9] The margin of error in both is very small; the temperature, for example, should be correct to within $20°$ or so at a temperature of somewhere between $600°$ and $700°$ C. This may have been judged by the removal of test pieces during the firing.

We have seen how numerous are the critical factors in the production of lustre: the correct recipe for the pigment; a glaze that softens the right amount at the right temperature; and a kiln that has a uniform distribution of heat and flow of gasses that can be precisely controlled for both temperature and

[6]Bahrami (1949a, p. 97, pl. 10) shows kilns from Gurgan, and (1947a, pp. 225–9) from Kashan. Similar kilns are found at Siraf and Nishapur, and elsewhere.
[7]Abu'l-Qasim actually mentions no refractory medium, which is used in all later recipes—see Caiger-Smith (1973, passim). Caiger-Smith in a letter to the author suggested that residue from the grinding of the metallic ores may have provided a suitable material.
[8]Allan (1973, para. 27). An interesting fact about the method of stacking the tiles for the lustre firing is revealed by the occurrence on the reverse of many star tiles of an imprint in a darkish pigment of the design of another tile. This imprint is never central but is offset to a greater or lesser degree (see Plate 5). This suggests that the tiles were stacked in the kiln resting one against the next, probably on their edges. The imprint must be transferred during the firing, but as the glaze does not soften to any considerable degree, there is no danger of the tiles sticking together. This manner of loading the kiln is paralleled exactly by the practice of the lustre potters in Italy in the mid-sixteenth century, as described by Piccolpasso (1980, pp. 87–8).
[9]Caiger-Smith (1973, pp.26, 59 and 72).

5   Reverse of a TILE, showing ghost image from adjacent piece acquired during firing.
Diameter 20 cm (7.8 in)
Metropolitan Museum of Art, New York, 41.165.17. See page 34

atmosphere. With all these variables, potential faults are numerous. According
to Caiger-Smith the most common faults are the four following: underfiring,
overfiring, uneven firing and 'red-flashing'. Underfiring results in only a pale
non-reflecting lustre stain on a glaze that has not sufficiently softened at the
temperature reached. Overfiring results in a dull and thin lustre, because the
copper has become volatile and been carried off with the kiln gasses. In
extreme cases the earth medium will adhere to the over-soft glaze, and give a
dull non-lustrous finish. In red-flashing the copper becomes slightly volatile
and stains the glaze round the design, the effect varying from a pinkish flush
along the lines of the design, seen in Colour Plate J, to a deep-red stain that in
extreme cases all but obliterates the original painting. This is thought to be
caused by a combination of overfiring and unsatisfactory draught, possibly

accentuated by the presence of water vapour in the kiln. Uneven firing results from one part of a piece becoming hotter than another, or subject to a greater flow of gasses, either of which will affect the colour of the final lustre.

All these faults can be seen on Persian lustres. The lustre pigment will only degrade with the actual decay of the glaze surface, and so on those pieces where the lustre is faint (often described as 'faded') but the glaze is in good condition, one of the first two faults is probably the cause. Red-flashing is not rare, though for some reason it tends to occur more often on tiles than on vessels. The uneven firing is naturally more noticeable on large objects, in particular on tiles, though it is common to find that the outside of a vessel is a different colour from the inside. The baking-in of the earthy medium may account for those wares which have a brown lustre with no metallic reflections.

In a few rare instances, the lustre technique is found together with enamel *minai* painting. When successful the effect can be very splendid, but it appears that the combination was risky.[10] In many examples the lustre is very uneven or appears not to have taken at all (Plate 56). This suggests that the temperature and atmosphere required by the two methods of decoration were difficult to match. Successive firing may have been required for each technique—thus increasing cost and risk of wastage for the potter. Pieces exist, however, in both miniature (Plate 57) and Kashan style (Plate 56), which possibly indicates that a small number of pieces were produced over a number of years.[11]

[10]Pope (1939, pl. 705 and 706), Washington (1973, no. 46) and Paris (1971, no. 49). This last piece shows lustre clearly on the reverse; on the front the lustre has hardly taken.
[11]See below, page 84.

Chapter 4

ATTRIBUTION TO PRODUCTION SITES

Three major styles of lustre painting have been identified on wares of the pre-Mongol period. Two of these styles are conventionally attributed to the town of Rayy, and the third to the town of Kashan. At least two other sites are regularly cited as production centres in the same period—Sava and Gurgan—and wares of the Il-Khanid period are often attributed to Sultanabad. The products and styles of painting of these last three sites are not clearly defined.

It is the thesis of this study that this 'accepted' view is not correct, and that all the lustre wares of both pre-Mongol and Il-Khanid periods are the product of one centre—Kashan—and that the stylistic differences reflect not different centres but differing traditions and sources of design. The story is one of stylistic synthesis, not rivalry.

Before we examine what evidence is available for the attribution of lustre wares to different sites, let us review the current accepted version of events and see how the story was built up. In his discussion of the Persian lustre wares of the Godman Collection, Henry Wallis illustrated in 1891 a 'waster' that had been found in the ruins of the city of Rayy (Plates 6 and 7),[1] and this attribution was adopted for virtually all lustred ceramics, until the work of A. U. Pope and Richard Ettinghausen in the 1930s. In this decade, the separate products of Kashan were identified, leaving Rayy as the source of two other distinct styles.[2] Sava was also suggested as a site, though the identification of its wares was less than certain.[3] In the mid-1940s material began to emerge from the ruins of the old city of Gurgan, and although this material resembled closely that of Rayy and Kashan, Gurgan was adopted as a fourth centre.[4] The

[1]Wallis (1891, pl. XXIX, fig. 8).
[2]Ettinghausen (1936b).
[3]Pope (1939, pp. 1625–31).
[4]Bahrami (1949a); see also Anon. (1947), Bahrami (1947b) and Ades (1949).

37

Sultanabad region had long been quoted as a source of a particular kind of Il-Khanid slip- and underglaze-painted pottery, and lustre wares in a roughly similar style tend to be attributed to the same site.[5]

The three major styles are known as the 'Rayy monumental', the 'Rayy miniature' and the 'Kashan'. The monumental style is that derived from Egyptian sources, as we have seen in a previous chapter. The miniature style is so-called both from the scale of the drawing and its derivation from manuscript painting styles. The main characteristic of the Kashan style is the closely textured surface, where the lustre ground is scratched through with a series of tiny commas. The two Rayy styles were thought to be the earliest, produced from shortly before 1179 (the earliest date found on Persian lustre ware) until the destruction of the city by the Mongols in 1220. Kashan was considered a rival school which started production in about 1200, but survived the Mongol onslaught and continued to produce wares (along with Sultanabad) during the Il-Khanid period. Gurgan also was thought to have started about 1200, but like Rayy to have succumbed to the Mongols. Sava was supposed to have been in production from the 1180s, judging from the dates on *minai* bowls found there.[6]

Before we review the evidence on which this story rests it is perhaps worthwhile to make two points of a general nature. First, when dealing with luxury wares, the numbers of sherds reported found on a site are no sure indication of local production. Such wares were made to be traded, and large cities would import the articles they required from whatever source. Fragments of lustre ware are found on sites all over Persia; a large number of bowls were discovered in the excavations at Ghazna, in Afghanistan; and the finds from Gurgan in the north-east of Persia probably represent the stock of a merchant trading them in the area. In the west, fragments were found at Hama in Syria, at Fostat in Egypt, in Constantinople, and one fragment was even dug up in the garden of the Alhambra palace in Granada, Spain.[7] Virtually all the material known to us from Persia has been dug up by commercial diggers, and their reports of the quantities found at particular sites reflect perhaps more their diligence or the ease of excavation rather than any more historically enlightening fact.[8]

---

[5]In the publication of his collection in 1910, Kelekian gives Sultanabad as the find-spot of many of his lustre pieces. Unlike other authors, he wisely refrains from assuming that they were made there.

[6]Such a thesis is constructed in Pope (1939), Lane (1947) and other general works.

[7]For the pieces found at Ghazna see U. Scerrato, 'The First Two Excavation Campaigns at Ghazni', *East and West*, X, 1959, p. 49; for those from Syria see P. J. Riis et alii, *Hama, Les Verreries et Potteries Médiévales*, Copenhagen, 1957, pp. 120–7; for those from Fostat see G. T. Scanlon, 'A Note on Fatimid-Saljuq Trade', *Islamic Civilisation, 950–1150*, ed. D. S. Richards, Oxford, 1973, pp. 265–74. The piece from the Alhambra is held in the Museum of that palace and is unpublished.

[8]Understandable reluctance to reveal the sites of profitable or illegal excavations has certainly led to deliberately misleading attributions.

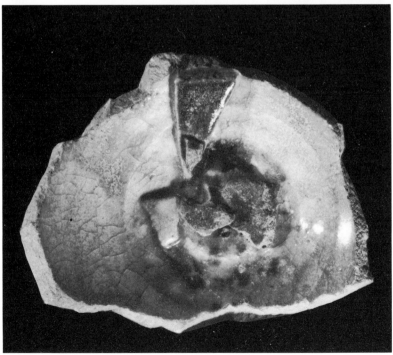

6, 7   SHERD. Miniature style, length 10.5 cm (4.1 in)
British Museum, 91,10–20,13. See pages 37 and 40

Secondly, the term 'waster' has been much abused. In any firing a kiln will inevitably produce some damaged and unsaleable wares, and the heaps of such rejects found in a place are a sure sign of local manufacture. Only a large number of defective pieces found on a site, or pieces very badly damaged—e.g. several pieces stuck together—can unequivocally point to a manufacturing site. The finding of one spoilt piece is of much less significance. Flaws, the distortion of walls, splashes of coloured glazes from other vessels, jagged pieces broken from adjoining vessels and fused into the glaze in the firing; none of these things alone necessarily rendered a vessel unsaleable, for all are found on whole and otherwise perfect pieces. In the case of 'lustre wasters' the fault has often occurred in the first firing, yet the piece has still been considered sufficiently valuable to decorate with lustre and refire.[9]

Rayy is the centre which has longest been considered a production site for lustre wares. It was the first site from which sherds were collected, and it had special appeal for Victorian scholars since it was identified as the site of the apocryphal Rhages (Tobit, 4:1). The 'waster' in the British Museum (Plates 6 and 7), published in 1891, seemed conclusive.[10] Further wasters are mentioned by Pope in the *Survey* (though not illustrated),[11] and, in spite of the reattribution of a great body of material to other sites in that work, Rayy is generally credited with the production of the two earliest styles of lustre painting.

On closer examination, Rayy's credentials appear decidedly weak. The damage to the British Museum's 'waster' consists of small pieces of another vessel stuck to the inside of what was originally a bottle or jar (Plate 7). From what remains of the piece it appears that the walls were not distorted and the glaze only scarred on the inside. The outside appears unharmed. It is almost certain that the damage occurred in the first firing, when the glaze became fluid and allowed the fragment, fallen from another piece, to adhere. If this is the case, the damage was evidently so slight, or indeed not noticed inside the closed form, that the jar was painted and refired. This solitary piece can hardly be considered worse than a second, and certainly it is not sufficient ground alone for the attribution of the ware. The other 'wasters' mentioned by Pope have never been illustrated, and it is not even clear that he is referring to wasters of lustre ware. The sherds from the Rayy excavations preserved in Persia and America contain no lustre wasters, though wasters of other types of ware do occur.[12]

As elsewhere, the quantity of lustre ware sherds found at the site is no real indication of provenance, for Rayy was one of the largest cities in Persia and

[9]For example, the random drops of coloured glaze on the dish in Colour Plate E and on many others, and the perfectly preserved but distorted pieces illustrated by Bahrami (1949a, pl. 8).
[10]See note 1.
[11]Pope (1939, p. 1567, note 3).
[12]One fragment of a monochrome frit waster is in the University Museum, Philadelphia, and part of a mould for frit wares is in the Museum of Fine Arts, Boston.

stood at the crossing of the country's two major trade routes. It is to be expected that it was a major importer and handler of luxury goods, whatever their source. Ettinghausen argued in 1936 that collections of sherds from Rayy showed such a preponderance of 'Rayy' styles that their manufacture there could reasonably be assumed.[13] However, excavations at Rayy also uncovered large numbers of Kashan-style pieces. The fact that slightly larger numbers in 'Rayy' styles were also found does not indicate a local production. The town of Rayy was largely destroyed, not by the Mongols in 1220, but earlier by the inhabitants themselves. Sectarian violence in 1186 resulted in members of the Shi'ite sect, about half of the population, fleeing the city. Further clashes between different orthodox sects depleted the population still more, and whole quarters of the city were abandoned. The contemporary writers Yaqut and Ibn al-Athir describe the city as largely in ruins before the arrival of the Mongols.[14] The sectarian clashes took place before the Kashan style had developed, and we can assume that as a result of the depopulation demand for luxury ceramics declined, and with it the number of imported Kashan pieces.

In short, there is no firm reason other than habit for attributing the manufacture of lustre ware to Rayy.

Kashan on the other hand, provides us from a variety of sources with a wide range of indications which show that it was a major producer. Yaqut, writing in 1220, praises Kashan's ceramic wares, which he says were exported far and wide.[15] Indeed, it is thought that the Persian word for a tile, *kashi* or *kashani*, is derived from the name of the town.[16] Well-authenticated wasters of various wares, including three badly fired lustre bowls painted in the same style, have been found in Kashan together with the remains of kilns.[17] Inscriptions on the wares themselves provide further evidence. Ali and Yusuf of the Abu Tahir family both include the *nisba* (indicating their town of origin) *al-Qashani*, as does Yusuf's brother Abu'l-Qasim. A third lustre potter uses the form *al-Kashi*, while a fourth includes after his signature the phrase *al-muqim bi-Qashan* 'dwelling in Kashan' (Colour Plate G).[18] It is of no mean significance that this phrase is used by the only recorded lustre potter who has a *nisba* other than one relating to Kashan (see page 43). Mention of the town itself occurs in inscriptions on star tiles dated 738–9/1338–9 (page 142). It was from evidence such as this that Richard Ettinghausen first identified and described in detail

---

[13]Ettinghausen (1936b, note 20). This argument was countered by the author (1976) before he had seen the Rayy material in the United States. The amount of Kashan-style material at Rayy suggests that the historians may be exaggerating the extent of its destruction.

[14]P. Schwartz, *Iran im Mittelalter*, Leipzig, 1925, V, pp. 772–4.

[15]Yaqut (1866–73, IV, p. 15).

[16]*Encyclopaedia of Islam*, Leiden, 1st ed., under 'Kashi'.

[17]See in particular Bahrami (1947a) and Pope (1937, pp. 161–6).

[18]The spelling with either 'Q' or 'K', and the abbreviated form of the *nisba* 'al-Qashi' for 'al-Qashani' are accepted variants; see *The Encyclopaedia of Islam*, Leiden, 2nd ed., under 'Kashan'.

the characteristics of the 'Kashan style'. He was happy at that time to leave the other styles to Rayy.[19]

Sava can be easily dealt with. Pope suggests that it is a production centre on the grounds that two 'wasters' of tenth-century lustre were found there, that quantities of material were excavated there, and that two *minai* bowls found there bear a signature apparently with the *nisba al-Kashani*.[20] The two wasters, if of any worth at all as indicators of lustre production, are irrelevant to production in the pre-Mongol period. The quantities of material, apparently including further wasters (though probably of non-lustred pottery), have never been published, and in any case would be expected in the ruins of a once large and prosperous city. The question of the *nisbas* on the *minai* bowls, even if they existed, need not detain us long. Pope argues that they would not be needed in the home town, and therefore they indicate that the artists were working away from home. However, in the first place, works designed for export may be reasonably thought to bear a home-town *nisba*; in the second place, *nisbas* were certainly used in the home town, as inscriptions on buildings amply indicate.[21] When defining a distinct style, Pope himself remains cautious: '. . . a combination of Rayy and Kashan elements and an ensemble effect that does not quite accord with either probably indicates a Sava product'. In the years since the publication of the *Survey*, in spite of the number of new objects known, the Sava products are as elusive as ever. It would seem profitable to abandon the attempt to demonstrate a centre of lustre production in that city.

Sultanabad is a modern town, in whose dependent villages a large number of Il-Khanid slip- and underglaze-painted wares were said to have been found. By stylistic analogy large numbers of Il-Khanid lustre vessels were given the same attribution. It now seems probable, and is generally accepted, that all are the products of Kashan, and the term 'Sultanabad' has, since the publication of Lane's *Later Islamic Pottery*, been reserved as a convenient label for certain types of Il-Khanid non-lustred ware alone.[22]

Gurgan (more properly spelt Jurjan) is the latest candidate to be put forward. In the mid-forties a large number of lustre-decorated vessels were found by commercial diggers packed in large jars and buried in the ruins of the ancient city of Gurgan (modern Gunbad-i Qabus), and since then more jars have been

---

[19]Ettinghausen (1936b).
[20]Pope (1939, pp. 1625–31). For these bowls, which in fact do not show the *nisba al-Kashani*, see below page 70, and Watson (in press (a)).
[21]See, for example, contemporary instances in A. Godard, *Athar-e Iran*, I, 1936, pp. 56, 89 and 96.
[22]Lane (1957, pp. 6–13).

found periodically.[23] The pieces, preserved in pristine condition, excited much interest, and in 1949 a large number were published by the Persian scholar Mehdi Bahrami. He assumed that they were local products, arguing the large number of pieces found there, a number of wasters and a distinctive style of decoration. Arthur Lane, in his review of the book, remarked that all the vessels belonged to either the Kashan or Rayy styles and suggests that they were probably the stock of a merchant, buried before the Mongol invasions devastated the city in 1220 and not subsequently recovered.[24] He points out that the 'wasters' are not sufficiently distorted to be so regarded and that their excellent state of preservation (they are all whole pieces) suggests that they were buried along with the others for safe keeping. The matter of a 'distinct' style is not conclusive either. Those pieces in a 'Rayy' style are indistinguishable from similar pieces found elsewhere. Those in a 'Kashan' style, however, show a consistent manner which some have maintained is distinct from that of Kashan wares found on other sites. Yet the Gurgan 'manner' is completely in accordance with the Kashan style and has no elements that cannot be paralleled on other Kashan pieces. The apparent unity is explained by the fact that within the Gurgan finds occur several groups of almost identical examples of a number of the simpler Kashan designs. This is consistent with the theory that they were the stock of a merchant which would, in all probability, have included pieces ordered in bulk from a single workshop. Finally the epigraphy of the pots does not support a local attribution. A section of a large mihrab from a mausoleum in the city bears the (incomplete) signature of Ali ibn Muhammad ibn Abi Tahir with the *nisba al-Qashani*; a bowl dated 601/1204 is signed by a potter with the *nisba al-Qashi*; and most eloquent of all, a bowl, very characteristic of the general run of Gurgan finds, bears the signature of the potter Muhammad ibn Muhammad of Nishapur with the phrase *al-muqim bi-Qashan* 'dwelling in Kashan' (Colour Plate G).[25]

Excavations were conducted in Gurgan for a number of years in the 1970s, and though quantities of lustre sherds have been found, no direct evidence of local lustre production has been revealed.[26] Until positive evidence to the contrary is produced the material in Gurgan must be regarded as imported.

In short, the evidence for the attribution of lustre wares to Kashan is overwhelming, while evidence for attribution to other sites is meagre in the extreme. Given the technical complexities and the indications in the previous

[23]See note 4, and more recently Kiani (1974).
[24]Review in *Oriental Art*, II, 1950, pp. 164–5. Ernst Kühnel, in his review of the same book in *Ars Orientalis*, I, 1954, pp. 225–6, also remained unconvinced of a separate centre of production in Gurgan.
[25]Watson (1976, p.5) and (1979), Bahrami (1949a, pp. 91–2, 127, pls. 5, XLVIII and XLIX).
[26]These were directed by Dr Yusuf Kiani, who maintains that lustre ware was produced at Gurgan. Nothing this author saw of the excavation materials while in Persia convinced him of local production. Interim reports of the excavations have been too general to allow any judgement (e.g. M. Y. Kiani, 1974, pp. 126–33), but we await the final report with great interest.

history of lustre production that the technique was held as a monopoly, it is perhaps to be expected that in Persia too it was a monopoly held by a single centre.

It is largely because of the variety of styles of painting that different sites have been sought for its manufacture. However, the different styles can be closely related, and a history of their development can be suggested which sees them not as separate schools but as differing traditions which achieve a synthesis. It is in this light that the styles of lustre painting will be analysed and their development explained and, in the course of this study, other evidence linking the 'Rayy' and Kashan styles of painting will be presented. In the present state of our knowledge we are able to identify with certainty only one site—Kashan—as a producer of lustre ware.

Chapter 5

THE MONUMENTAL STYLE

The monumental style is so called because of its characteristically large-scale motifs and the bold manner of depiction. Its essential quality lies in the manner of painting: the motifs are shown reserved in white against a ground of lustre. It would appear that the designs were painted in thin outline first, then the background filled in with the lustre pigment, leaving the (usually) white glaze to act for the main motif of the design. Details are painted in lustre within the white areas.

A typical design shows a single large figure filling the major part of the decorated area, while in the background curls a scroll of fleshy palmettes. Outer borders of sketchy arabesques (painted rather than in reserve) frequently occur, as does the half-moon border on the rim (Plates 8–10). While large-scale motifs show the style at its most dramatic, they are not obligatory. In the famous 'School scene' dish from the David Collection (Plate 11a, b), the individual figures are all rather small, yet the manner of depiction remains the same.

Differing in approach are a large number of pieces, usually of less painstaking quality in the painting, in which the area is divided into panels and friezes, then filled with small motifs depicted in reserve, or with painted arabesques and scrollwork (Plates 17, 21 and 22). In one small class freely drawn arabesques alone cover the surface of the vessel (Plates 13 and 25). While reserved decoration is, as we have seen above, derived from Egyptian wares, it is interesting to note that there is no use of ornament scratched through the lustre, in spite of the widespread occurrence of this technique in Egypt.[1]

The range of subjects is not large. Horsemen occur fairly frequently, while seated figures, drinking or merely sitting, are perhaps the most common. The Berlin eagle (Plate 8) shows animal drawing in this style at its finest, the tense power of the bird accentuated by its claws thrust firmly through the border.

[1] Lane (1947, pls. 26a, 27a).

45

8 DISH. Monumental style, diameter 35.8 cm (14.1 in)
   Museum für Islamische Kunst, Berlin, I.1592. See pages 45, 48 and 52

The winged horse in Plate 9, by contrast, performs a graceful pirouette within its confines. In the Freer jug (Plate 27) an indeterminate breed of canine chases a somewhat pig-like hare. The motif of chasing animals occurs elsewhere as a border design (Plate 28). A small number of more particular and individual designs receive careful and skilled attention. The 'School scene' (Plate 11a, b) shows in the centre a master, rod in hand, surrounded by his class of children holding alphabet-boards on which are written simple combinations of letters. Seated immediately above the master, two children turn to face each other, which suggests that this may illustrate the first meeting at school of Laila and Majnun, whose unhappy love story was given its most famous rendering by Nizami in 1188–9; perhaps the dish was made soon afterwards. We have no means of telling whether two other splendid dishes, one showing an enthroned monarch with attendants (Colour Plate B), the other a warrior with sword and shield fighting off a leopard (Plate 12) are meant to represent specific epic

9 DISH. Monumental style, diameter 20.5 cm (8 in)
Metropolitan Museum of Art, New York, Rogers Fund, 16.87. See pages 45, 46, 52 and 67

10 DISH. Monumental style, diameter 23 cm (9 in)
Museum für Islamische Kunst, Berlin, I.1506. See pages 45, 48 and 67

stories or have more generalized associations. No attempt is made by the painters to suggest any real setting for the figures which might help us to decide. The scrolls bear no relation to any plant form, and can hardly have been meant to suggest a particular environment. Occasionally 'props' are scattered amongst the scrollwork. As in Egyptian wares, these sometimes take the form of jugs or ewers floating in the background, suggesting a scene of revelry and feasting (Plate 32). The 'School scene' has a jug, a bookstand and a number of alphabet-boards, though the master with stick and board in hand, alone seems to take notice of them (Plate 11a, b). In the throne scene the monarch is provided with cushions to sit on and rest against, but no other accoutrements or furnishings (Colour Plate B). The sun alone tells us he is seated out-of-doors. In spite of this abstract location, the figures do relate to one another by lines of sight and their gestures. In the better-drawn pieces the artist achieves a remarkable feeling for the depth and fullness of the figure, and considerable sensitivity of expression and pose (Plates 10, 14 and 32). The light, quick lines with which these illusions are created reveal that the artists are painters of considerable skill and dexterity—no hack copyists. The naturalistic quality of the figures stems from certain types of Egyptian lustre-painted pottery, as does the style of painting in reserve.[2] While many elements of the monumental style can thus be seen to stem from Egyptian decorative traditions, the facial features do not. These show the round 'moon' faces, small fine features and long locks which conform to the classic canon of Persian beauty which can be traced back to pre-Islamic Central Asian Buddhist sources.[3]

The narrow range of subjects is complemented by a limited number of decorative conventions and secondary motifs. Coats of animals and decoration of clothes are usually rendered by groups of dots, often in threes, of varying sizes (Plates 4, 10–12, etc.). The large palmettes and half-palmettes that break up the background are characteristic of this style. The simpler versions could well be from Egyptian sources, but the fleshier types with more articulated inner leaves find their closest parallel in contemporary Quranic manuscript illumination of Iraq and Persia.[4] Other scrollwork varieties appear to be the potters' independent versions. Very common is a half-palmette scroll where the palmettes are depicted with a single stroke of the brush. This occurs as a border motif (Plate 8), and also appears, generally in a rather disintegrated form, in dividing and pendant motifs (Plates 28 and 30) and within panels and cartouches (Plates 19, 21 and 24). Closely related is sketchy scrollwork with a smaller and finer texture. This occurs in garment decoration and border design, where it is often used as the background to a pseudo-inscription (Colour Plates A and B). Another characteristic element is a circular, jewel-like

[2]Lane (1947, pl. 27b), Grube (1976, nos. 88, 89).
[3]A. S. Melikian Chirvani, 'Le Bouddhisme dans l'Iran Musulman', *Le Monde Iranien et l'Islam*, II, 1974, esp. p. 37; see also Melikian Chirvani (1967) and Chapter 6, note 5.
[4]A. J. Arberry, *The Koran Illuminated*, Dublin, 1967, pl. 25.

11a   DISH. Monumental style, diameter 48 cm (18.9 in)
     David Collection, Copenhagen, 50/1966. See pages 45, 46, 48 and 52
11b   Detail of Plate 11a.

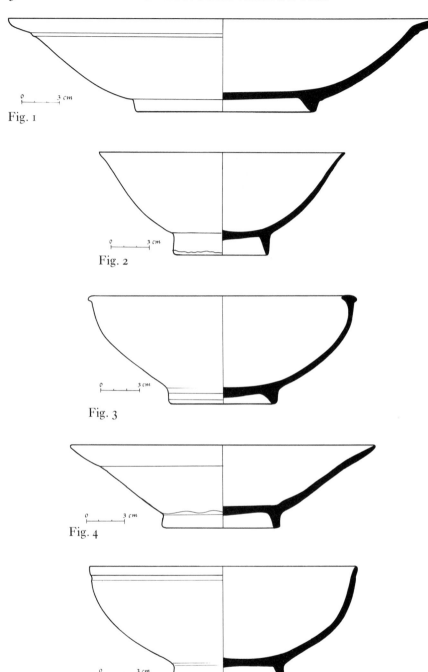

Fig. 1

Fig. 2

Fig. 3

Fig. 4

Fig. 5

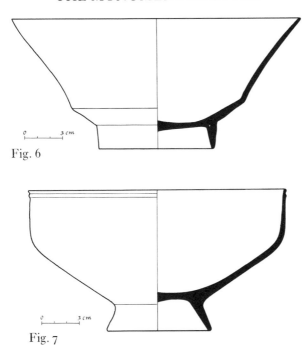

Fig. 6

Fig. 7

Fig. 1 Profile of monumental style dish, Victoria and Albert Museum, 54–1907. *See page 52, Plates 4, 8, 11–13 and Colour Plate B*

Fig. 2 Profile of monumental style bowl, Victoria and Albert Museum, C25–1918 *(Plate 14). See pages 52 and 67, Plates 15, 17–20*

Fig. 3 Profile of miniature style bowl, Victoria and Albert Museum, C776–1909. *See pages 80 and 104, Plate 38. A similar shape is decorated in the Kashan style, Plate 87*

Fig. 4 Profile of a dish decorated in the Kashan style, Victoria and Albert Museum, C163–1977 *(Plate 68). See pages 80 and 104. A similar shape is decorated in the miniature style, Plates 39–47, and 64–5*

Fig. 5 Profile of a bowl decorated in the large-scale miniature style, Ashmolean Museum, 1956–28 *(Plate 50). This shape is also decorated in the miniature style, see pages 80 and 104, Plates 43 and 49. A similar shape is decorated in the Kashan style, Plates 62, 66, 67*

Fig. 6 Profile of a bowl decorated in the Kashan style, Victoria and Albert Museum, C162–1977 *(Colour Plate G). See pages 67, 80 and 104, e.g. Plates 70, 71.* The 'conical' bowl.

Fig. 7 Profile of a bowl decorated in the Kashan style, Victoria and Albert Museum, C161–1977. *See page 104 and Colour Plate F*

motif to which this scroll often acts as a background (Plates 11, 17 and 30). Inscriptions play only a small part in the decoration. A band of often largely illegible cursive script, usually based on series of conventional blessings to the owner, often runs round the exterior of a bowl or dish (Plate 20a), while pseudo-inscriptions of which virtually only the tall *hastae* of the definite article remain, occur in border decorations (Plates 9, 16 and 27). Only rarely is a more legible inscription, often in the squarer Kufic script, used as a major part of the decoration, and in these cases the pieces usually reflect an Egyptian prototype (Plates 15 and 16).[5] A typical text reads: 'Lasting glory, prosperity, happiness, liberality, generosity, and long life perpetually to the owner' (Plate 15).

Only one piece in the monumental style is signed, and one bears a dedication. The signature is that of a certain Abu Tahir ibn Muhammad Hamza ibn al-Hasan, possibly the first recorded member of the Abu Tahir family, and it occurs on a hemispherical bowl decorated in modest fashion with inscriptions and panels of arabesques (Plate 16).[6] The dedication occurs on a fragmentary octagonal tray, decorated on a pale-blue glaze with a single figure and an inscription round the rim and the outside of the well: '. . . Sun of the Arabs, Provost of the Kingdom, Umar ibn Ahmad al-Tusi.'[7] The personal dedication is all the more surprising in that the piece, made for some unidentified official originating from the town of Tus in north-eastern Persia, is of indifferent quality.

The coloured glaze of this piece is also unusual. It is common to find the backs of dishes and bowls coloured a uniform deep blue through the application of a transparent cobalt glaze, and footrings and bases of bowls and jars are also often blue-glazed. Less common is an overall application of the dark-blue glaze (Plate 35); the pale blue, an opacified cobalt glaze, is much rarer (Plate 20 a, b). A uniform turquoise glaze, though used previously in Egypt, is not found amongst Persian lustres; however, the surface of a piece may be divided into radiating panels of white, blue and turquoise (Plates 22 and 23). On occasion, blue is used to outline cartouches (Plate 17).

Two vessel shapes in particular characterize the monumental style. The first is the large flat dish (Colour Plate B, Plates 4, 8, 11–13 and Fig. 1) which stands on a wide low footring, and whose cavetto rises to a narrow flat rim. The second is the smaller bowl (Plates 14, 15, 17–20 etc. and Fig. 2) whose walls rise from a cylindrical footring, curving upwards before flaring outwards. Both these shapes are characteristic to the point of being diagnostic, for they are not found decorated in either the miniature or the Kashan style. The first is perhaps derived from an Egyptian shape, where a hemispherical bowl also has a similar wide footring and narrow rim. The flaring bowl is inspired by Chinese porcelain shapes.

[5]E.g. Grube (1976, nos. 97 and 98).
[6]Fehérvári (1981, no. 111).
[7]Stern (1963).

12   DISH. Monumental style, diameter 35.2 cm (13.8 in)
     Keir Collection. See pages 46, 48 and 52
13   DISH. Monumental style, diameter 36.7 cm (14.4 in)
     Ades Family Collection. See pages 45 and 52

14　BOWL. Monumental style, diameter 19 cm (7.5 in)
　　Victoria and Albert Museum, C25–1918. See page 48
15　BOWL. Monumental style, diameter 18 cm (7.1 in)
　　Ades Family Collection. See page 52

16 BOWL. Monumental style, signed by ABU TAHIR IBN MUHAMMAD HAMZA IBN
    AL-HASAN, diameter 22 cm (8.6 in)
    Khalili Collection. See pages 52 and 178
17 BOWL. Monumental style, diameter 20 cm (7.8 in)
    Ades Family Collection. See pages 45 and 52

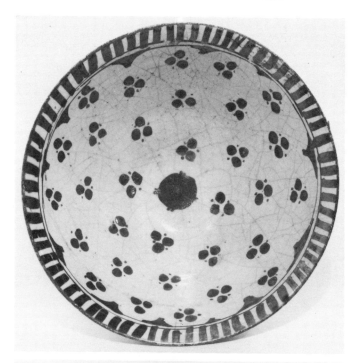

18   BOWL. Monumental style, diameter 18.7 cm (7.3 in)
Courtesy of Sotheby's. See page 67

19   BOWL. Monumental style, diameter 14.7 cm (5.8 in)
Ades Family Collection. See page 48

20a, b   BOWL. Monumental style, on a blue glaze, diameter 18.5 cm (7.3 in)
Louvre, MAO 485. See page 52

21   BOWL. Monumental style, diameter 19 cm (7.5 in)
     Ex-Kelekian Collection. See pages 45, 48 and 67
22   BOWL. Monumental style, radiating panels of white, turquoise and blue glaze,
     diameter 15.8 cm (6.2 in)
     Courtesy of Sotheby's. See pages 32, 45 and 52

23   BOWL. Monumental style, radiating panels of blue and white glaze,
   diameter 17.5 cm (7 in)
   Dar al-Athar al-Islamiya, Kuwait National Museum, LNS 15C. See pages 32 and 52
24   SWEETMEAT DISH. Monumental style, diameter 33.5 cm (13.3 in)
   Walters Art Gallery, Baltimore, 48.1011. See pages 33, 48 and 67

25   JUG. Monumental style, height 14.5 cm (5.7 in)
     Victoria and Albert Museum, C186–1928. See pages 45 and 67
26   JUG. Monumental style, height 12.5 cm (4.9 in)
     Victoria and Albert Museum, Clement Ades Gift, C36–1978. See page 67

27 JUG. Monumental style, height 17.9 cm (7 in)
Courtesy of the Freer Gallery of Art, Smithsonian Institution, Washington D.C.,
09.370. See pages 46, 52 and 67

28 JUG. Monumental style, height 27.5 cm (10.8 in)
Victoria and Albert Museum, C1954–1910. See pages 46, 48 and 67

29   ALBARELLO. Monumental style, height 18.5 cm (7.3 in)
     Victoria and Albert Museum, 369–1892. See page 67
30   BOTTLE. Monumental style, height 25.7 cm (10 in)
     British Museum, 1928, 7–21,11. See pages 48 and 67

31   EWER. Monumental style, height 37 cm (14.5 in). The cock's head spout may be from a different, but similar, piece
Victoria and Albert Museum, C160–1928. See pages 33 and 67

32   BOTTLE. Monumental style, height 25.5 cm (10 in)
Ex-Kelekian Collection, Cincinnati Art Museum. See pages 48 and 67

33 BOTTLE. Monumental style, height 20.3 cm (8 in)
   Courtesy of Sotheby's. See pages 33 and 67
34 BOWL. Monumental style, diameter 13.5 cm (5.3 in)
   Victoria and Albert Museum, C1232–1919. See pages 33 and 67

35 DISH. Monumental style, on a blue glaze, diameter 23 cm (9 in)
    Courtesy of Sotheby's. See pages 33, 52 and 67
36 BOWL. Monumental style, diameter 15.6 cm (6.1 in)
    Ades Family Collection. See pages 33 and 67

The monumental style is also found on a variety of other shapes: an angular dish on a tall foot (Plates 9 and 10); a bowl with vertical walls (Plate 21); globular handled jugs with varying sizes of neck (Plates 25–8); albarellos (Plate 29); bottles (Plates 30 and 32); sweetmeat dishes (Plate 24); and a number of lobed forms (Plates 33–6). The cock's-head ewer (Plate 31) is a rarity. Metalwork has provided the inspiration for a number of these and other shapes, in particular the handled jars or jugs and those pieces with lobed or angled walls. One sees but a few reminiscences of previous ceramic traditions in Persia in either shape or design. The bowl with vertical walls (Plate 21) may be a refined version of a shape that appears in twelfth-century sgraffito wares from the Garrus region,[8] while the design consisting of scattered groups of three dots takes us back to the earlier slip-painted wares of Nishapur and eastern Persia (Plate 18).[9] A common feature of the majority of the monumental style shapes is a tendency to 'looseness' in the potting. The contours are often rather imprecise, even irregular, angles tend to be rounded and footrings not turned neatly. This is particularly seen among the closed forms (Colour Plate A, Plates 28–30), which stand in marked contrast to the tauter shapes and more sharply articulated potting of many of the miniature and Kashan style pieces.

The few tiles painted in the monumental style will be discussed in a later chapter, as will the figures.

There is no internal evidence for the dating of the monumental style, though a certain amount of circumstantial evidence ties its history closely to that of the miniature style, which can be more precisely dated. There is no reason to assume that the style was in production much before or after the dates that can be given to the miniature style, which lie roughly in the last quarter of the twelfth century. Such a hypothesis gives the most plausible account of its relations with both miniature and Kashan styles. It also fits what we can deduce of the history of wares in other techniques, and in particular the 'silhouette' technique and the development of underglaze painting. Through its vessel shapes the silhouette technique, in which a black slip is carved away against a white ground, is closely connected with the ateliers that produced the monumental style. They share the same flaring bowl shape (Fig. 2). The silhouette technique can be shown to have been replaced by underglaze painting in about the year 1200, when the flaring bowl is abandoned in favour of the conical bowl (Fig. 6) characteristic of the Kashan lustre style which was adopted at about the same time. It would seem that the silhouette technique, the monumental lustre style and the flaring bowl were all abandoned when the Kashan style developed at the very end of the twelfth century.[10]

[8]Cf. R. Schnyder, 'Mediaeval Incised and Carved Wares from North West Iran', in *The Art of Iran and Anatolia*, Percival David Foundation Colloquy No. 4, University of London, 1974, fig,. G/4.
[9]C. K. Wilkinson, *Nishapur*, New York, 1973, Group 5, nos. 14, 25, 38.
[10]O. Watson, 'Persian Silhouette Ware and the Development of Underglaze Painting', in *Decorative Techniques and Styles in Asian Ceramics, Colloquies on Art and Archaeology in Asia, No. 8*, University of London, 1979, p. 92.

Chapter 6

THE MINIATURE STYLE

The miniature style differs from the monumental in many respects: in painting technique, in motif, in approach to decoration and in vessel shape. It is properly to be regarded as a separate school. However, a number of shared elements and borrowings show that the two styles are closely related.

The essence of the style lies in the technique of painting, for the motifs are painted with the pigment directly on to the glaze; only in a few motifs borrowed from the monumental style does the design stand in reserve on a lustre ground. Two approaches to decoration are found. In the majority of pieces, the surface is divided into a number of friezes and panels, each filled with small repeating motifs (Plates 37–46, Colour Plate C). Much less common, and usually of finer quality, are those pieces where a single large motif dominates the design; they may be termed large-scale miniature style (Plates 48–50, 52).

The range of motifs is even smaller than that used in the monumental group. Horsemen and seated figures combined with a variety of plants and arabesques provide by far the greater part of the designs (Plates 37–9, etc.). Animals occur as a border motif borrowed from the monumental style (Plates 38, 40 and 42); the caravan of camels on the fragment from Sèvres is exceptional (Plate 40). The painting is carried out in a rapid sketchy style, in which the features of the face and other small details are often confused and lost. The clothes, on the other hand, often receive more detailed treatment, with decoration of stripes, arabesques and palmettes being on occasion the most lovingly depicted (Plates 39 and 40). The landscape which these figures populate is invariably formed by small chequer-board trees and long single stems bordered on each side by a row of dots representing small leaves or blossoms (the 'dotted' plant). Equally characteristic of the style are a number of the subsidiary motifs. An arabesque mesh formed by hatched lozenges flanked by pairs of birds in silhouette occurs frequently in both panels and friezes (Plates 45 and 53) and is used to cover the entire surface of a dish (Plate 43). A chain-and-stripe motif is used in a variety

37   VASE. Miniature style, dated Muharram 575/June 1179, height 14 cm (5.5 in)
British Museum, 1920, 2–26, 1. See pages 24, 26, 68, 80 and 197

of forms, often in the lowest register of a design (Plate 46) or, branching into split-palmettes, as a dividing motif (Plate 47). A motif combining pendant triangular elements with an arabesque spray is more commonly used as an alternative to the chain-and-stripe motif in the lowest register (Plate 42 and Colour Plate C), as is a rather random scroll (Plate 47). Some pieces have main elements made up of cartouches with riders or seated figures in the monumental style, and the uncertainty as to which category they belong to underlines the close connection between the two styles (Plate 47). Other minor characteristics, including a blue-glazed reverse, are also shared by the two styles.[1] Inscriptions in the miniature style are written with more serious intent than in the monumental. In addition to the stylized or pseudo-inscriptions and conventional blessings to the owner, quatrains in Persian are found, similar or identical to those occurring on later Kashan style pieces (see page 152). Dates and signatures occur a number of times and will be discussed below (page 80).

The total effect of these elements combined together is lively, but tends to be somewhat confused. The style is not as common as the monumental, and it

[1]The blue-glazed reverse of miniature style pieces is very much rarer than in the monumental style.

is probable that it was developed not primarily for lustre, but for the *minai* enamelled technique, whose various colours resolve the detail better. Many *minai* pieces are painted in an identical style.[2] The confused impression given by many of the lustre pieces perhaps led the potters to develop a larger scale of design in which a single image is used. For the most part the motifs follow those of the smaller-scale style—seated figures and horsemen (Plates 49 and 50). They are painted in the same way, though with more care and detail, as befits their larger size. The same chequer-board trees and dotted plants occur, but additional elements are an awning or section of sky above, and an indication of a fish-filled stream or pond below.

One quite exceptional bowl shows a remarkable scene (Plate 49) of the entry of a potentate into a town. The dignitary is mounted and is accompanied by other mounted attendants and a bodyguard on foot carrying two spears. He is entering the town through a complicated gateway from which two men watch with great suspicion. Behind them four veiled but eagle-eyed ladies seem more excited at the prospect. The inscription is unread and may give some clue as to the event taking place. These large-scale miniature style bowls are closely related to a group of bowls in the *minai* technique known as the 'Muharram' bowls, from the name of the Islamic month that occurs in the dates of three of them. Five dated 'Muharram' bowls are known, two dated 582/1186 and three 583/1187 (Plate 51), which provides us with a rough date for the lustre pieces.[3] The two groups share many elements of design, the chequer-board tree, the dotted plant, the awning and pool and a band of inscription beneath the main scene (Plates 49 and 50). The group of 'Muharram' bowls can be attributed to Abu Zaid on the basis of his signature found on one of them. Abu Zaid was responsible for at least one similar bowl in lustre, of which unhappily only a rim-sherd bearing his signature survives.[4]

The source of inspiration for the miniature style is manuscript illustration. We are lucky that a manuscript survives of the story of *Warqa and Gulshah* dating from the pre-Mongol period, and richly illustrated. Its exact place of production is a matter of some dispute, but it is certain that it represents the style current in Persia immediately before the Mongol invasions. In it we find the same small figures with round faces, long locks and elaborately patterned garments; and trees and plants from which the chequer-board tree and dotted plant evidently derive.[5] The long, low horizontal format of the book painting is translated on the pottery into narrow friezes and panels.

---

[2]Pope (1939, pls. 656–99).

[3]Pope (1939, pls. 686–9).

[4]Watson (1976, pl. 12). See pages 84–5. The *minai* bowls were attributed to Sava by Pope on the basis of the *nisba al-Kashani* found on one of them. In fact none have any such *nisba*, see Watson (in press (a)) and page 42.

[5]A. S. Melikian Chirvani, 'Le Roman de Varque et Golšah', *Arts Asiatiques*, XXII, 1970, esp. colour plates on pp. 98–9, and figs. 13, 15, 16 etc.

38   BOWL. Miniature style, dated Safar 587/March 1191, diameter 38 cm (14.9 in)
Courtesy of the Art Institute of Chicago, 1927.414. See pages 68, 80 and 197

One piece is of particular interest in that it shows a very strong Egyptian
influence in its design (Plate 48). It is a dish with a flat base and low flaring wall
standing on a high foot. By its shape, its hard dense body and thick glaze it
would seem to be a very early piece. The design shows a donkey bearing a
woman in a howda, the background filled with birds in silhouette, random
leaves and sprays of dotted plants, surrounded by an inscription border of
blessings in Kufic script. The birds, plants and the figure of the woman are in
the miniature style, but the Kufic inscription and the donkey come straight
from Egypt.[6]

[6]Cf. Grube (1976, no. 41).

39   DISH. Miniature style, dated Jumada I 590/May 1193, diameter 54 cm (21.2 in)
     Khalili Collection. See pages 68, 80 and 197
40   SHERD OF A DISH. Miniature style, height 19.5 cm (7.7 in)
     Musée de Sèvres, Paris. See pages 68 and 80

41 DISH. Miniature style, diameter 33.1 cm (13.1 in)
Brooklyn Museum, New York, L.68.46.3, courtesy of Sotheby's. See pages 68, 69 and 80
42 SPOUTED JAR. Miniature style, height 15 cm (5.9 in)
Victoria and Albert Museum, C362–1918. See pages 68 and 80

43   BOWL. Miniature style, diameter 14.8 cm (5.8 in)
     Ades Family Collection. See pages 68 and 80
44   JUG. Miniature style, height 12.6 cm (4.9 in)
     Ades Family Collection. See pages 68 and 80

45 EWER. Miniature style, height 26.7 cm (10.5 in)
Courtesy of Sotheby's. See page 68

46   BOTTLE. Miniature style, height 30 cm (11.8 in)
     Keir Collection. See pages 68 and 69

47 BOTTLE. Miniature style, height 25 cm (9.8 in)
Victoria and Albert Museum, C1230–1919. See page 69

48   DISH. Large-scale miniature style, diameter 19.5 cm (7.7 in)
     Ades Family Collection. See pages 68 and 71
49   BOWL. Large-scale miniature style, found at Ghazna, diameter 21.7 cm (8.5 in)
     Kabul Museum, 63.2.1. Photograph: Frances Mortimer. See pages 68 and 70

50 BOWL. Large-scale miniature style, diameter 21.3 cm (8.4 in)
    Ashmolean Museum, Oxford, 1968–28. See pages 68 and 70
51 BOWL. Enamelled in *minai* technique, large-scale miniature style, dated
    583/1187, diameter 21 cm (8.2 in)
    British Museum, 1945, 10–17,261. See pages 70 and 84

The miniature style is found on a wide variety of shapes of bowls, dishes and jars; none however are as characteristic of the style as are the bowl and dish of the monumental style. A deep bowl with flaring sides that turn vertical before ending in an overhanging rim (Plate 38, Fig. 3) is found a number of times, and appears to have been adopted from earlier sgraffito clay wares of the so-called Aghkand type, produced in the twelfth century in north-western Persia.[7] Also occurring fairly frequently are a dish with flaring walls and a barely articulated rim (Plates 39–41, Fig. 4), a hemispherical bowl on a low footring (Plate 43, Fig. 5), and a saucer with wide flat rim standing on a high foot (Plate 52). A variety of bottles and jars are found, many of them recorded in only single examples. The jug (Plate 44) and 'posset pot' (Plate 42) occur more frequently. Conical bowls, characteristic of the Kashan style, are also found (Fig. 6). We cannot tell whether they date from after the introduction of the Kashan style, or are prototypes for the Kashan shape. The tiles and figurines decorated in miniature style are discussed separately (pages 118 and 123). Concern over the subtleties of profile is often more marked in these wares than in those of the monumental style. Shapes are more carefully thrown and turned and a generally better finish is achieved.

The inscriptions on miniature style wares provide us, in addition to the quatrains and blessings mentioned above, with four dated and two signed pieces. The earliest dated piece is a fragmentary vase in the British Museum (Plate 37). The poem on it reads:

> Oh Heavenly sphere, why do you set afflictions before me?
>   Oh Fortune, why do you scatter salt on my wounds?
> Oh Enemy of mine, how often will you strike at me?
>   I am struck by my own fate and fortune.

> May joy, exultation and cheerfulness be with you,
>   May prosperity, happiness and triumph be your companions.

and the date follows '. . . on the third day of the year five hundred and seventy five/10 June 1179'.[8] Two pieces are dated 587/1191, the large bowl in the Chicago Art Institute (Plate 38), and the fragment of a vase whose whereabouts is now unknown signed by the potter Abu Zaid 'in his own hand' (Plate 53). The next date Jumada I 590/May 1194 occurs on a large and elaborate dish (Plate 39). The second signed piece, by the same potter as the first, and followed by an incomplete and illegible date, is a rim-sherd of a bowl decorated in the large-scale miniature style.[9]

---

[7]R. Schnyder, op. cit., fig. H/2.
[8]Gyuzalyan (1966). The inscription, contrary to Fehérvári's remark (1973, p. 85, n. 2) does not state that the piece was made in Rayy.
[9]Watson (1976, pl. 12).

52   DISH. Large-scale miniature style, diameter 22 cm (8.6 in)
     Ades Family Collection. See pages 68, 80 and 88
53   SHERD OF A VASE. Miniature style, by ABU ZAID and dated 587/1191
     After Bahrami (1949), present whereabouts unknown. See pages 68, 80, 180 and 197

54   BOTTLE. Miniature style, dated 595/1199, height 25.5 cm (10 in)
     Museum für Islamische Kunst, Berlin, I 46/70. See pages 84 and 197
55   SHERD OF A DISH. Kashan style, dated Dhu'l-Hijja 595/September 1199
     British Institute of Persian Studies, Tehran. See pages 84, 109 and 197

56 DISH, with both *minai* enamel and lustre painting. Diameter 22 cm (8.6 in)
    Louvre, MAO 440. See pages 36 and 85
57 FLOWER VASE, with both *minai* enamel and lustre painting. Height 23 cm (9 in)
    Walters Art Gallery, Baltimore, 48–1278. See pages 36 and 85

The next date found on lustre wares is 595/1199 which occurs both on a bottle in Berlin-Dahlem and on a rim-sherd in the collection of the British Institute of Persian Studies in Tehran. The bottle is difficult to place (Plate 54). The upper half is decorated with a sketchy scrolling motif which is found as a minor filling device on all three styles, monumental, miniature and Kashan, though it is most widely used in the monumental style. Beneath the inscription band occurs a type of chain-and-stripe motif that is found on miniature as well as Kashan style pieces. The inscription is scratched through a band of lustre, a practice found only on Kashan pieces. This mixture of motifs perhaps reflects the fact that it was made at a time of change, when the third major style was being developed. In the last month of the same year is dated the rim-sherd (Plate 55), of which enough of the design remains for it to be classed as Kashan style—the double row of inscriptions, one scratched, one painted, and, most significantly, the scratching of clusters of commas through the background lustre of the main field. This is the earliest datable Kashan style piece, and, from this date onwards, the only dated pieces are in the Kashan style. Some dozens of dates are recorded in the first two decades of the thirteenth century. One is justified in assuming that the Kashan style developed in the last few years of the twelfth century, and became the dominant one. It would be too simple a story to assume that the monumental and miniature styles were immediately discontinued. It is probable that pieces in these styles were produced alongside those in the new style, but how many and for how long we have no means of telling: though surely the great creative energy that went into decorating vessels and tiles in the new style rendered the earlier ones quickly outmoded.[10]

The potter Abu Zaid must be credited with much of the impetus behind the change in style. The range of his signed works in the Kashan style shows his high status as a potter in that period. His signatures on pieces in the miniature style—the only ones that occur—show his skill as a potter at a much earlier date. The *minai* bowls he made are his earliest dated works, yet they are perhaps among his best (e.g. Plate 51). They are of great importance in showing his long involvement in the miniature style and, through him, that style's close connection with the Kashan. They also amply demonstrate the close association of the *minai* and lustre ateliers. That both products were made in the same workshops by the same potters is further indicated by the rare group of pieces with decoration in both techniques.[11] The lustre on the Louvre

[10]The miniature style certainly carried on in *minai* wares, as dated pieces of 604/1207 (Iran Bastan Museum, Tehran) and 616/1219 (Keir Collection) show. See Bahrami (1946b, p. 113) and Grube (1976, no. 143). A lustre bowl dated 601/1204 from Gurgan is in a form of the miniature style, but of unorthodox design for lustre wares. It much more resembles a typical *minai* design, see Bahrami (1949a, p. 126) and cf. Lane (1947, pls. 68b, 69b). It stands as an oddity.
[11]See above, page 36, note 10. These wares are to be distinguished from those pieces which have *underglaze* or *in-glaze* pigments as well as lustre (see page 33). Pope (1939, pp. 1556–7) has caused confusion by referring to such pieces as 'polychrome lustre', which has been taken by some to mean a combination of lustre and *minai*, e.g. Fehérvári (1973, p. 93, no. 105).

dish with a horse-rider can now only be seen in the background to the rim inscription (Plate 56), though on the reverse it is better preserved. Traces remain on the front which show that the horse was intended to stand against a lustre-decorated ground. The vase in the Walters Art Gallery, Baltimore, has a scratched inscription in a lustre band round the rim (Plate 57). This may indicate a date after 1200 when such inscriptions became common in the Kashan style. There are again traces of lustre, though very faint, elsewhere on the body. It would appear that the potters had difficulty in controlling the two techniques on a single piece. A fragment in the Islamic Museum, Berlin, also painted in the miniature style, shows how splendid the result could be when successful.

Chapter 7

THE KASHAN STYLE

_____

TRANSITION

Before looking closely at the Kashan style and its characteristics in detail, it is instructive to examine a number of pieces in which the potters were modifying the basic monumental and miniature styles. Instructive, because it indicates with what aspects of the style the potters were concerned, and shows the experiments which led to the formulation of the Kashan style.

In both monumental and miniature pieces the experimentation is concerned with the background. In a number of monumental style pieces the background is not filled in with lustre. Instead, the main motifs are outlined in a broad band of lustre, surrounded by an undecorated margin, and the ground round this is filled with closely textured sketchy scrollwork, in which float cartouches of broadly drawn arabesques (Plate 58, Colour Plate D). The concern of the artist was evidently to lighten the background, to relieve the ponderous effect of the plain lustered ground and bold palmette scroll. His problem lay in how to define the figure against the textured ground. The solution of the band of lustre and plain margin meant that the figure could still be shown in reserve, and not rely for its impact on the thin lines which are used for the initial delineation. Striking though these pieces are, the technique is clumsy, as the unsubtle bands detract from the fine drawing and make the figures sit like paper cut-outs on an unrelated ground. They were evidently not deemed a success and few were produced. Similar experiments with the background are seen in a few pieces in the miniature style. Here the concern was more probably to lend clarity to the designs and substance to lustre reflections, for in the miniature style there is a tendency for the designs to appear confused and the lustre sparse and spindly. On a fragment in the Louvre the background has been provided with small stippled contour panels (Plate 59), and on a piece in the Ades Family Collection all the background is covered with stippled scrolling, in this case also leaving a narrow plain margin round the figures

86

58   DISH. Transitional monumental style, diameter 42.5 cm (16.7 in)
     Metropolitan Museum of Art, New York, Fletcher Fund, 1932, 32.52.3. See pages 28
     and 86
59   SHERD OF BOWL. Transitional miniature style, length 13 cm (5.1 in)
     Louvre, MAO 449–203. See page 86

(Plate 60). Miniature style pieces with these modifications are also very uncommon and likewise cannot have been considered satisfactory. The solution, as we shall see when examining the Kashan style, lay in a scratching or sgraffito technique. This is seen, perhaps for the first time in Persian lustres, on the last mentioned piece.

THE KASHAN STYLE

As the experimental pieces discussed above suggest, it is in the treatment of the background that the Kashan style distinguishes itself most clearly. As in the monumental style, the figure is drawn in reserve on a lustre ground, which is relieved not only by the scrollwork seen also in the earlier style, but by a series of small spirals or commas scratched through the lustre to give it a lighter texture.

The Kashan style is designed expressly to show off the lustre technique at its most brilliant, and cannot be copied in other techniques. It owes little either to foreign schools of decoration (like the monumental style) or to decoration in other media (like the miniature style). Once established it lasted with little modification for almost a century and a half. Though limited in subject matter, the drawing at its best compares favourably with contemporary manuscript illustration for both composition and draftsmanship.[1]

The textured sgraffito background (as opposed to the painted texturing of the transitional pieces) is first seen on two dishes which in many respects relate to the earlier school but show the decisive stylistic break (Plates 61 and 62). The dish in the Fitzwilliam Museum (Plate 61) may be closely compared to a piece in the large-scale miniature style from the Ades Family Collection (Plate 52). They are of identical shape, and have the same interlocking device on the reverse. The border of running animals on the rim and the inner band is again identical on the two pieces. The Fitzwilliam piece, however, shows a horseman, in reserve, on a lustre ground broken up by half-palmette leaves and small scratched commas and thus is in the Kashan style. The second piece also shows a horseman, this time a falconer, and the background is even more decisively broken up by series of spirals (Plate 62). In many other respects, however, the piece might be classified as in the miniature style—from the shape of the bowl, the pendant motif on the reverse, and the type of inscriptions in the interior.[2] New, however, is the shape of the palmettes in the background—a type that is to become a feature of the Kashan style— and the concern for the all-over texturing of the design. It is interesting to note that both pieces stem from the miniature style, except that the main motif, a large figure shown in reserve,

[1]Melikian Chirvani (1967). His stylistic comparisons with ceramics are valid. The attribution of the manuscripts to Persia itself has been less readily accepted.
[2]Washington (1973, no. 29).

60   DISH. Transitional miniature style, diameter 16.2 cm (6.4 in)
     Ades Family Collection. See page 88
61   DISH. Kashan style, diameter 22.2 cm (8.7 in)
     Fitzwilliam Museum, Cambridge, C120–1935. See page 88

comes from the monumental style. This combination of elements from both previous schools confirms the interconnection of all three. The reminiscences of the earlier schools do not last long, and those potters working on the new style develop a new repertoire of subsidiary motifs, a new range of vessel shapes and a new decorative effect. The potter Abu Zaid seems to be the driving force of the new style, as we have seen, signing more pieces than any other potter, and signing the earliest of them. He was not the only skilful practitioner, however, for other potters, in particular Shams al-Din (Plate 63) and Muhammad al-Muqri (Colour Plate F), produced pieces in every way the equal of his. Abu Zaid's importance is seen in the numbers of his signed pieces, all of very high quality, and his activity, with Muhammad of the Abu Tahir family, as a producer of tiles (see page 124).

Tile production also developed at the same moment as the development of the Kashan style, whereas it had been very unimportant in the earlier period. Much of the finest Kashan work is on tiles, but we will for the time being confine ourselves to the vessels, and leave discussion of the tiles to a later chapter.

The dish with a polo player in the Victoria and Albert Museum epitomizes the new style (Colour Plate E). It is dated 604/1207, though it is not signed. Round the main motif runs a double line of inscription, one scratched through a lustre band, the other painted. The text is of quatrains in Persian, of an amorous nature, which typically bear no relation to the painting. The polo player is shown in large scale, painted in reserve on a lustre ground. The different areas of the design are distinguished by different patterning of various textures and densities, either painted or scratched through the lustre. The face alone, with its halo behind, is left plain. The half-palmettes and birds in the background are one of the most characteristic features of the new style. The half-palmettes, virtually semicircular in shape, are articulated inside by a row of dots and a few hatched lines. The plump birds have similar detailing. A plate in the University Museum, Philadelphia, shows a central motif of two figures sitting together surrounded by a broad frieze consisting of these half-palmettes and birds alone (Plate 64), while another dish substitutes for this an elaborate Kufic inscription (Plate 65). A bowl in the Metropolitan Museum shows a seated prince with attendants (Plate 66). This piece exemplifies the artist's concern to texture the whole surface with differing patterns, leaving only the faces plain. The awning above and pool beneath have been seen before in the large-scale miniature style wares and the associated *minai* group. The physiognomy of the features is unchanged from the former styles, though the roundness of the face and fineness of the features become, if anything, more exaggerated.

Quite exceptional in design is the Freer Gallery plate, dated Jumada II 607/November 1210, which bears a dedication to an unidentified amir and is signed by Shams al-Din al-Hasani (Plate 63). It shows a horse attended by a sleeping youth and five other figures. In the pool beneath the scene swim a

62 BOWL. Kashan style, diameter 20 cm (7.8 in)
Courtesy of the Freer Gallery of Art, Smithsonian Institution, Washington D.C., 40.22.
See page 88

63 DISH. Kashan style, by SHAMS AL-DIN AL-HASANI, dated Jumada II 607/November
1210, diameter 35.2 cm (13.8 in)
Courtesy of the Freer Gallery of Art, Smithsonian Institution, Washington D.C., 41.11.
See pages 90, 98, 104, 108, 155, 181 and 198

64 DISH. Kashan style, dated Safar 608/July 1211, diameter 49.5 cm (19.5 in)
University Museum, University of Pennsylvania, Philadelphia, NE–P 19.
See pages 90, 98, 104 and 198

number of fish and a naked woman. The inscriptions do not help us to identify
the scene, for they consist of verses in Arabic and Persian, either of love poetry
or of conventional good wishes to the owner. It was first thought that the scene
was the Persian epic hero Khusrau first sighting his love Shirin as she bathed,
but there are iconographical objections to this. Shirin should not be completely
naked, and Khusrau should certainly not be asleep! In an extensive iconographical study Guest and Ettinghausen suggest a possible mystic interpretation, in which the fish in the water stand for the union of the mystic with
God, immersed in infinite Divine Grace; the woman for the earthly manifesta-
tion of Divine Beauty, and the horse and attendants as the earthly attachments
which the youth rejects in his mystic sleep and quest.[3] This interpretation is all

[3]Ettinghausen (1961).

65   DISH. Kashan style, diameter 49.5 cm (19.5 in)
Metropolitan Museum of Art, New York, Fletcher Fund, 32.52.2.
See pages 90, 98, 104 and 109

the more interesting in view of the nature of the poems on the tiles and the use to which they were put. This question will be considered again in Chapter 11.

Such a complex design is unique. As in the previous styles, by far the greater majority of designs consists of horsemen, seated figures, princes with attendants and animals, now mostly gazelles (Plates 67–9, Colour Plate G). Other animals occasionally make an appearance, such as dogs, lions, bulls and, exceptionally, an elephant (Plate 74). The setting for these figures is by and large as abstract as before, though trees, plants and pools more often now indicate a garden or outdoor scene. Inscriptions play a larger part in the decoration than before, and concentric bands of different types frequently surround a central motif (Plates 70–2). Cursive *naskhi* is both scratched through a lustre band and painted on the white glaze; the angular Kufic script is frequently developed into ornate friezes on a scrollwork ground, punctuated

66   BOWL. Kashan style, dated Jumada II 607/November 1210, diameter 30 cm (11.8 in)
     Metropolitan Museum of Art, New York, Gift of Horace Havermayer, 41.119.1.
     See pages 90, 98, 104, 108–9 and 198

on occasion by small cartouches (Plates 69 and 70). Figural ornamentation is
not mandatory: many pieces have their surfaces divided into panels and friezes
of inscriptions, arabesques and scrollwork alone (Plates 72 and 73). Subsidiary
motifs that occur regularly, apart from the half-palmette and bird described
above, include a large heart-shaped palmette and a chain-and-stripe motif (on
the lower body and the neck of the ewer in Plate 78), this latter somewhat
simplified from the version found in the miniature style. Both these motifs are
used in friezes and panels, and commonly on the lower parts of bottles and
ewers (Plates 77, 80 and 83) or on the reverse of bowls, where a bold stylized
Kufic inscription is also found (Plates 71 and 87).

67 BOWL. Kashan style, by ABU ZAID, dated 616/1219, diameter 21 cm (8.2 in)
    Escher Foundation, Haags Gemeentemuseum, The Hague, OC(I) 55–1932.
    See pages 93, 98, 104, 109, 180 and 199
68 DISH. Kashan style, diameter 21.5 cm (8.4 in)
    Victoria and Albert Museum, Clement Ades Gift, C163–1977. See page 93

69 DISH. Kashan style, diameter 30.5 cm (12 in)
Victoria and Albert Museum, Clement Ades Gift, C164–1977. See pages 93 and 94
70 BOWL. Kashan style, dated 614/1217, diameter 22 cm (8.6 in)
Victoria and Albert Museum, Clement Ades Gift, C160–1977. See pages 93, 94, 104 and 199

71   BOWL. Kashan style, dated Shawwal 614/January 1218, diameter 23.2 cm (9.1 in)
     Dar al-Athar al-Islamiya, Kuwait National Museum, LNS 210C.
     See pages 93, 94 and 199
72   BOWL. Kashan style, diameter 22 cm (8.6 in)
     Ades Family Collection. See pages 93, 94, 98 and 104

73   BOWL. Kashan style, diameter 27 cm (10.6 in)
      Ades Family Collection. See pages 94 and 104

    The Kashan style of painting is not found on coloured glazes, but details in
blue and turquoise are used more frequently than before. They do not just
outline cartouches and panels (Plate 72), but delineate the stems of scrolls
(Plate 77), the patterns on garments (Plate 67) and other such elements of the
design (Colour Plate G). The turquoise colour, tending to spread in indistinct
and blurred patches, is much less common than the blue and is used for
broader areas such as the foliage of trees. A remarkable bottle in the Freer
Gallery shows seated figures whose clothes are coloured in blue and turquoise
with overglaze *minai* black, while lustre is used to fill in the background.[4] It is
interesting to note that on the largest and best-quality pieces lustre alone is
used as though the better painters did not want to be restricted by pre-
determined areas and lines of colour (Plates 63–6, Colour Plates E and F).

[4]Washington (1973, no. 46).

74a, b   SAUCER. Kashan style, by MUHAMMAD IBN ABI NASR IBN AL-HUSAINI, dated
         Shawwal 611/February 1214, diameter 21.5 cm (8.4 in)
         Etchecopar Collection, after Bahrami (1949). See pages 93, 104, 108 and 181

75   SPOUTED JAR. Kashan style, height 13.3 cm (5.2 in)
       Ades Family Collection. See page 104
76   EWER. Kashan style, height 36.2 cm (14.2 in)
       Louvre, MAO 444. See page 104

77   EWER. Kashan style, height 17.3 cm (6.8 in)
     Ades Family Collection. See pages 94, 98 and 104
78   EWER. Kashan style, height 22.5 cm (8.8 in)
     Ades Family Collection. See pages 94 and 104

79   JUG. Kashan style, height 21.5 cm (8.4 in)
      Ades Family Collection. See page 106
80   JUG. Kashan style, height 34 cm (13.4 in)
      Museum für Islamische Kunst, Berlin, I 1/62. See pages 94 and 106

81   JUG. Kashan style, height 20.3 cm (8 in)
     Ades Family Collection. See page 106
82   EWER. Kashan style, height 34.5 cm (13.6 in)
     Ades Family Collection. See page 104

Apart from the intentional use of colour, some pieces have random splashes of blue or turquoise (Colour Plate E). Various explanations have been put forward for these—that they were intentional blemishes to ensure that 'only Allah is perfect', that they were intended to bring good luck, as turquoise is a lucky colour, or that they were merely the result of accidental oxidization of copper salts through a technical fault in the firing.[5] The technical explanation must be rejected, for the effect only occurs when the glaze itself contains copper, which here it does not. One is inclined to reject the first explanation, for the drops are not found on every piece, and the implicit arrogance, even blasphemy, that the piece would be perfect without an intentional blemish, must have been evident. Close examination of the colours shows them to be drops of coloured glaze, which must have fallen from other pieces fired in the same kiln during the first firing. Perhaps because of the beneficial nature of turquoise and blue colours in the Middle East, as agents which ward off the Evil Eye, small patches were deemed acceptable and did not consign the piece, already a costly object even before the application of the lustre, to the waster heap.

A wide variety of vessel shapes occurs. Some are new creations, others continue from the earlier period. The big dish with flaring sides (Plates 64–5, Fig. 4), the hemispherical bowl with low footring (Plates 66–7, Fig. 5) and the bowl with overhanging rim (Plate 87, Fig. 3) have been seen before, but not a deep rounded bowl on a spreading foot (Colour Plate F, Fig. 7). The conical bowl (Plates 70, 72, Colour Plate G, Fig. 6) becomes the most common shape, and though it occurs decorated in the miniature style, we cannot tell whether these are late examples on the new shape, or an old shape continued in the new style. Whatever its history, it is only with the Kashan style that the shape is extensively used. Flat dishes with lobed walls are taken from moulds, their shape inspired by metal trays. The dishes in Plate 63 and Colour Plate E are taken from the same mould, with twenty-nine lobes, and yet other examples from the same mould are known.[6] The mould must have lasted in this case at least three years (the two dishes illustrated are dated 1207 and 1210) and judging by the differing styles of painting on pieces taken from it, it must have been used by several painters who perhaps worked together for one potter in a large workshop. Such co-operation is known to have existed in the production of tilework. Metal prototypes can be traced for other shapes, such as the bowl with flaring and indented rim (Plate 73), the ewer (Plates 76 and 82), and the small saucer supported on three feet in the shape of harpies (Plate 74a, b). This last piece is decorated inside with a veiled woman riding on an elephant. The piece bears a signature which may possibly be that of Muhammad of the Abu Tahir family (see pages 108 and 181). The 'posset pot' and various spouted ewers occur (Plates 75–78); that from the Louvre (Plate 76) is decorated with

---

[5]Erdmann (1935) and Ettinghausen (1961, p. 63, n. 141).
[6]Ettinghausen (1936b, p. 62 and n.35) lists one underglaze and four lustre-painted dishes taken from this mould.

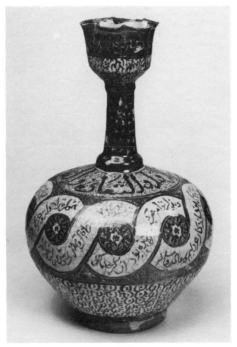

83   BOTTLE. Kashan style, height 24.5 cm (9.6 in)
     Victoria and Albert Museum, Clement Ades Gift, C165–1977. See pages 94 and 106
84   BOTTLE. Kashan style, height 19.8 cm (7.8 in)
     Ades Family Collection. See page 106

85   FLOWER VASE. Kashan style, height 17.9 cm (7 in)
Louvre, 5896. See page 106

intertwining snakes or dragons, whose heads confront one another on the
shoulder. The design is also known on a number of bowls.[7] Bottles with
various shapes of neck and mouth (Plates 83 and 84), jugs and tankards (Plates
79–81), and multiple-spouted flower vessels (Plate 85), often follow shapes
already seen in the miniature style. Large jars are known, some of considerable
size, with elaborate moulded decoration.[8] A unique piece is a small table in the
Philadelphia Museum of Art (Plate 86). Following some architectural type,
possibly a garden pavilion, each of its six sides is moulded in the form of a niche
with pointed arch, in the upper half of which sits a cross-legged figure, cup in
hand. At each corner are moulded triple arches, containing further narrow
pointed niches. The top, with border inscription, shows a scene of seated ruler
with attendants, while every part is decorated with designs of flying birds,
interlacings, scrollwork and arabesques.[9]

[7]Bahrami (1949a, pls. LXIII, LXXXVIII), E. J. Grube, 'The Art of Islamic Pottery', *Bulletin
of the Metropolitan Museum of Art*, February 1965, pl. 28 and Sotheby's *Islamic Sale*,
10 October 1978, lots 98 and 105.
[8]Bahrami (1947a, fig. 133).
[9]Cup-stands, which are relatively common in Syrian pottery (e.g. Lane 1947, pl. 60b; and
E. Grube, 'Rakka-Keramik', *Kunst des Orients*, IV, 1963, Abb. 4 and 5) are not found in Persia.
Small tables, mostly in the form of pavilions, occur in monochrome glazed pottery; see
M. Mahboubian, *Treasures of Persian Art after Islam*, New York, 1970, nos. 294 and 295; and
R. Ettinghausen (ed.), *The Islamic Garden*, Dumbarton Oaks, Washington, 1976, introduction
and text figures A and B, where he discusses their derivation from garden pavilion architecture.

86 a, b   TABLE. Kashan style, height 26 cm (10.2 in)
*Philadelphia Museum of Art, Gift of Henry P. McIlhenny in memory of his
parents, 143−41−1. See page 106*

The inscriptions that are found on the Kashan style pieces are for the most part verses, usually Persian quatrains, though Arabic verses have also been identified. The style and sentiment of these verses is repetitive, and the same poems occur on the lustre tiles. Discussion of their content and significance will be reserved for a later section (page 151). Generalized blessings to the owner, such as we have encountered before, are not infrequent, but dedications to particular individuals are very rare. The Freer dish with the possibly mystic scene (Plate 63), bears a dedication to an amir, for whom a string of titles is given but no name; this perhaps occurred on a missing section of the rim now restored in plaster. We are as little able to identify the vizier, al-Hasan ibn Salman, to whom a lustre jar from the Bahrami collection was dedicated.[10] These two pieces, together with a third in the monumental style mentioned above (page 52), are the only known dedications to individuals on lustre vessels. This should not surprise us, for even on the highly ornate and richly inlaid metal objects of the period dedications to individuals are very much the exception.[11]

DATES AND SIGNATURES

Of the seven signatures that have been recorded on lustre vessels of the pre-Mongol period, only one occurs more than once—Abu Zaid. His importance has already been commented on, and he will appear again in the discussion of the lustred tiles. It is perhaps of interest to point out here that he is the only identified tile manufacturer known for certain also to have made vessels. The signature on the elephant saucer (Plate 74) discussed above may be that of his partner Muhammad ibn Abi Tahir but signatures of the rest of the Abu Tahir family occur only on tiles and do not appear elsewhere. The numbers of signed vessels known is extremely small—only thirteen pieces in the entire pre-Mongol period, and none for certain in the Il-Khanid period. Artists such as Shams al-Din al-Husani, who made the Freer plate (Plate 63) and Muhammad ibn Abi al-Hasan al-Muqri, who signed one piece (Colour Plate F) and possibly a second, were consummate artists, and the paucity of their documented pieces belies their skill. There seems to be no discernible reason for the signature of a potter to appear on a pot; certainly it was not the skill of the craftsman that decided it, for Muhammad ibn Muhammad al-Nishapuri (Colour Plate G) and Muhammad ibn Abi Mansur al-Kashi both signed fairly ordinary pieces, while masterpieces such as the Victoria and Albert Museum dish (Colour Plate E) and the Metropolitan Museum of Fine Art bowl (Plate

[10]Bahrami (1949a, pl. 11, p. 134).
[11]See, for example, A. S. Melikian Chirvani, *Le Bronze Iranien*, Musée des Arts Décoratifs, Paris, 1973, pp. 20–69.

87 BOWL. Kashan style, dated 615/1218, diameter 20 cm (7.8 in)
Victoria and Albert Museum, C1233–1919. See pages 94, 104 and 199

66) are unsigned, and other fine dishes are both unsigned and undated (e.g. Plate 65). It is tempting to suggest that the inclusion of dates and signatures was decided for as banal a reason as the amount of space left at the end of the other inscriptions. If this were the case the 'filling-in' priorities would seem to be date first and signature after, for dates are much commoner: almost sixty dates occur on vessels in the Kashan style between 595/1199 and 624/1226. A study of the dated pieces (see page 189) reveals a certain pattern of production, though the chance survival of the 'Gurgan' finds and a group of wasters in the Iran Bastan Museum in Tehran inevitably distort the picture, and we must be cautious of accepting it at face value. The span of the Kashan style, however, seems fairly clearly marked. The earliest date Dhu'l-Hijja 595/September 1199, is found on a sherd (Plate 55). The next date, Rajab 598/April 1202 is found on a dish with lobed cavetto signed by Abu Zaid.[12] Large numbers of dated pieces are not found until 604/1207 (e.g. Colour Plate E) but they then continue unabated until 616/1219 (Plate 67). Four dated pieces alone are known between then and 624/1226, when a gap occurs for some thirty-five years. The wares that are produced after this date are discussed below. It would seem then that the main period of production in the Kashan style took place between the early years of the thirteenth century and the end of the second decade. Within this period it is noticeable that the finer and more sophisticated pieces occur in the first half, while simpler and more speedily executed wares were made throughout the period, their numbers increasing in the latter part.

[12]Most of the interior design on this dish may not be the original, but a replacement from another dish or tile, see Bahrami (1946b, figs. 1 and 2).

Chapter 8

IL-KHANID WARES

The disruptions to the economic and social life of Persia caused by the Mongol invasions led to a steep decline in the production of lustre ware. A number of dated tiles shows that the potters did not abandon their craft entirely, but no dated vessels are known between 624/1226 and 660/1261 and there is no reason to suppose that any were made. The resumption of tile production on a large scale in the 660s/1260s is accompanied by the making of vessels, though by no means on the same scale as in the pre-Mongol period. Very many fewer of them appear to have been produced, most energy going into the production of tiles, and their character has changed. The painting, as seen also in the tiles, is simplified and stylized; the vessel shapes are no longer thin and finely contoured, but heavy and often ungainly. New shapes are seen, in particular those taken from imported Chinese celadons and porcelains, which, thanks to the greater ease of trade between the Chinese and Persian Mongol states, had arrived in the west in greater numbers than before. The Chinese derivation of two forms characteristic of the Il-Khanid lustre wares is seen in the bowl of hemispherical form which often has petal panels on the reverse (Plate 88 and Colour Plate H), and in the large dish with articulated rim (Plate 89).

The influence of Chinese design is apparent in the occasional phoenix or dragon, and the lotus makes its first appearance.[1] The source of these images is probably not ceramics, but Chinese silks, and their impact on Islamic decoration as a whole in the thirteenth and fourteenth centuries was profound.[2] For the greater part the designs are adaptations of those found in the pre-Mongol period: seated figures (Plates 90a, b and 91), animals (Plates 92 and 93), and panels and friezes of arabesques with animals and other formal motifs (Plate 94 and Colour Plate H). The designs have a charmingly naive air. The

---

[1]These motifs are commoner on tiles than on vessels (see Colour Plate L) and on vessels in other techniques than lustre, see Lane (1957, pls. 1, 3, 4 and 6).
[2]Lane (1957, p. 1ff).

88   BOWL, profile of Colour Plate H. Il-Khanid period, diameter 21.5 cm (8.4 in)
       Victoria and Albert Museum, C1955–1910. See page 110

figures are stiff and doll-like, with disproportionately large heads (Plates 90a, b
and 91), the foliage has often the plain border and filling of 'peacock eyes',
or veining of a single line ending in a dot (Plates 89a, b, 90a, b, and 93).
Characteristic are panels of interlocking 'S' motifs (Plate 94, Colour Plate H),
stylized inscriptions (Colour Plate H) and arabesques or palmettes. Bowls, jugs
and dishes are commonly found; rarities are the large jars, one covered with
eleven rows of hexagonal panels, each decorated in the manner of a tile with a
human figure or animal (Plate 95), and a piece of similar shape with friezes of
humans and animals in relief (Plate 96).

The dated pieces show that most of the Il-Khanid lustre vessels were made
in the 660s/1260s (three examples) and 670s/1270s (five examples), and
production dwindled during the 680s/1280s (two examples). One name is
mentioned, supposedly painted on the reverse of a small dish (Plate 91): Umar
Ali (= Amal-i Ali 'work of Ali'?) but the reading of this has been queried.[3]

Lustre decoration for vessels had become by this time somewhat outmoded
and more interest was shown by the potters in the development of new
underglaze-painted techniques—the so-called Sultanabad wares—which
despite their technical differences show great stylistic dependence upon the
lustre tradition.[4]

[3]This piece was no. 48 of the Kelekian Loan to the Victoria and Albert Museum, which was
returned to the owner in 1952. In the Ceramics Department Library's copy of Kelekian (1910),
Arthur Lane, by the illustration of the piece (pl. 48) comments on the name Omar Aly:
   'No such thing, only a sketchily drawn flower. Pope repeats the mistake in the *Survey of
   Persian Art*. There is *no* signature or date on this piece. Checked in 1948.'
[4]Lane (1957, pp. 6–13, pls. 1–4).

89 a, b   DISH. Il-Khanid period, dated 667/1268, diameter 28.5 cm (11.2in)
David Collection, Copenhagen, Isl. 96. See pages 110, 111 and 200

90 a, b   DISH. Il-Khanid period, diameter 47.5 cm (18.7 in)
Courtesy of the Freer Gallery of Art, Smithsonian Institution, Washington D.C.
09.111. See pages 110 and 111

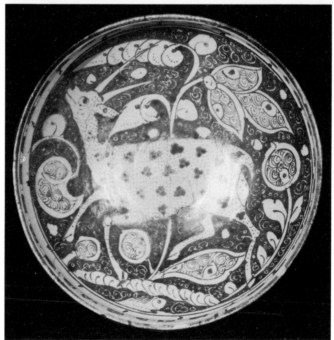

91   DISH. Il-Khanid period, diameter 15 cm (5.9 in)
     Dar al-Athar al-Islamiya, Kuwait National Museum, LNS 301C. See pages 110, 111
     and 182
92   DISH. Il-Khanid period, diameter 18 cm (7.1 in)
     Dar al-Athar al-Islamiya, Kuwait National Museum, LNS 301C. See page 110

93   JUG. Il-Khanid period, height 21.5 cm (8.4 in)
     Ades Family Collection. See pages 110 and 111

94   BOWL. Il-Khanid period, diameter 20.5 cm (8 in)
     Victoria and Albert Museum, C755–1909. See pages 110 and 111

95   JAR. Il-Khanid period, height 68.5 cm (26.9 in)
      Private Collection. See page 111
96   JAR. Il-Khanid period, height 78 cm (30.7 in)
      Hermitage. See page 111

Chapter 9

FIGURES

While tiles and 'crockery' formed by far the greater part of the lustre potters' production, a small group of figures dating only from the pre-Mongol period are amongst the most interesting, and in some ways the most problematic, of their wares. A wide range of different types is known, the most common being small models of lions or bovines. They are all hollow, in general made up from moulded or simply fashioned parts. The lion is generally shown in a rather dejected and slumped sitting position with its head hanging low (Colour Plate I). In the middle of his back occurs a small spout with a ring handle. The cow or bull model (there is no means of verifying the sex) also occurs in a standard form and looks altogether happier (Plate 97). The cylindrical body is supported on four cylindrical legs and stands on a square base. The horns curve towards each other and meet where a palmette or similar device rises from the middle of the forehead. The long muzzle is open at the end, and a small spout on the back is connected by a strap handle to the back of the neck. These two designs occur in several examples of differing sizes and details, and are also recorded in other decorative techniques. In larger figures the modelling becomes more ornate — the tail of the bull turns into a snake or dragon,[1] and the horns and palmette are more precisely and carefully detailed. The bull from Seattle is perhaps the most spectacular of the lustred figures, for it bears on its back not a simple spout but a complete flower-jar supported by two small figures facing outwards with uplifted arms (Plate 98). Round the shoulder of the jar and on the flanks of the animal are subsidiary spouts. These two animals do not exhaust the range of lustred figures, but virtually all other models are known only in single examples. Birds are represented by the magnificent hawk in the Fitzwilliam Museum (Plate 99) and, if it can be classified as a bird, by the enormous harpy in the Metropolitan Museum.[2] A number of human figures are known,

[1] Grube (1976, no. 181).
[2] Grube (1966, fig. 2).

97   AQUAMANILE. Monumental style, height 18 cm (7.1 in)
Ades Family Collection. See page 117

including a bearded man seated with cup in hand (Plate 100), and a mother
suckling her child.[3] The cat (Plate 101), also in the Fitzwilliam Museum, is
distinguished by its realistic modelling.

Lustre painting in all three styles—monumental, miniature and Kashan—
occurs on these figures and all must date from the pre-Mongol period. They
are coated with either an opaque white or a transparent dark-blue glaze. The
approach to the decoration varies. In some pieces crude palmettes and scrolls
are used to emphasize the structure of the animal's body, differentiating the
flank from rump and shoulder (Colour Plate I); in other examples the body is
covered with a random series of panels decorated with scrolling motifs. A
number of pieces are covered in panels or cartouches containing little figures of
mounted horseman, seated figures or flying birds (Plates 98 and 99). The
human figures are given a schematic rendering of patterned garments (Plate
100).

[3]Lane (1947, pl. 53a); for a discussion of these models, see E. Kühnel, 'Ein Madonnenmotiv in
der Islamischen Kunst?', *Berliner Museen, Amtliche Berichte*, 1914; and M. Rogers, 'On a
Figurine in the Cairo Museum of Art', *Persica*, IV, 1969, pp. 141–79.

98 AQUAMANILE. Kashan style, height 44.5 cm (17.5 in)
Seattle Art Museum, Eugene Fuller Memorial Collection, 38.139. See pages 117 and 118

99   FIGURE OF A HAWK. Monumental style, height 47 cm (18.5 in)
     Fitzwilliam Museum, Cambridge, C1–1967. See pages 117 and 118
100 FIGURE OF A SEATED MAN. Monumental style, height 19 cm (7.5 in)
     Ades Family Collection. See page 118

The function of the figures is in many cases obvious. The bulls, with spout
on the back and an open muzzle, were intended as aquamaniles, their contents
of wine or water to enter through the back and be distributed through the
muzzle. The lions, with but a single spout, must have functioned as bottles.
The Seattle bull, with its multiple spouts, must have been intended as a flower
vase. The use of other pieces is more puzzling. Small figures with no openings
but with flat bases may have been used as bath rasps, a practice that is well
documented for later periods. Others, such as the bird figures, appear to have
been purely decorative: indeed, given the fragility of the material and the
impracticality of the slender handles on the larger aquamaniles, it may well be
the case that all the models were essentially decorative.[4]

[4]Watson (1981).

101   FIGURE OF A CAT. Monumental style, length 19 cm (7.5 in)
      Fitzwilliam Museum, Cambridge, C164–1946. See page 118

In the present state of our knowledge we cannot with any certainty say why these particular animals were chosen, and what, if any, precise association they had. The lion and bull have obvious astrological connotations, representing both beneficial signs in their own right as Leo and Taurus, and also as the domicilia of benevolent planets—the Sun and Venus respectively. There is evidence that popular beliefs gave the harpy and hawk similar beneficial powers. The human models may have been dolls or, as Dr Grube suggests, they may have functioned as amulets and charms.[5] As with so much of the symbolic interpretation of images in Islam, we are left, in the absence of secure documentation, to speculate freely.

[5]Grube (1966) and (1976, esp. pp. 199, 201, 228 and 239–45).

Chapter 10

TILES

There are three main types of lustred wall tiles: the 'mihrab' (directional niche) or tombstone tile, the frieze tile, and the star and cross tile. The mihrabs include the most complex structures attempted by the potters. In large mihrabs upwards of forty individual tiles may be used to construct a panel, usually in the form of a series of enclosed blind niches and friezes (Plates 104a, b, and 120). Smaller units are constructed simply from two to four tiles standing one on top of the other (Plates 113 and 126) and are here called 'medium mihrabs'. Single tiles, termed 'small mihrabs', sometimes occur in pairs (Plate 125 and Colour Plate N). The design of the 'medium' and 'small' mihrabs may resemble that of the inner sections of 'large' mihrabs, and in certain cases may originally have formed part of such a mihrab: surviving sections of large mihrabs indicate that large numbers have been dispersed. The inscriptions on some of them, and their position in the buildings they decorate, show that many are in fact tombstones rather than mihrabs; the term mihrab is here employed as a convenient label. Frieze tiles are square or rectangular in shape and usually bear a projecting upper cornice with moulded design and a moulded inscription in the main field (Plates 112 and 116, Colour Plate L). They were designed to surmount panels of dado tiles which ran around the inner walls of buildings (Plate 105). They are identical in form to the outer inscription friezes of large mihrabs and we cannot tell to which type an individual piece may have belonged. Smaller friezes without cornice decoration were used either as parts of large mihrab constructions or to cover the sides of tombs.[1] Star tiles, most commonly alternating with cross tiles of either lustre or monochrome glaze decoration (Plates 110 and 121, Colour Plates K and M), were used in dado panels or to cover tomb structures. Not all are eight-pointed, though this is the standard shape; others are six-pointed (Plate 115), octagonal (Plate 105) or hexagonal (Plate 114), but these are more rarely found.

---

[1] See in particular Kratschkovskaya (1946), and the friezes without cornices from Natanz, unpublished, see Watson (1977, p. 107).

122

The sizes of the tiles vary from scheme to scheme. The largest of the large mihrabs, that of 734/1334 (Plate 120), measures 3.28 metres (129.2 in) high, the smallest, that of 640/1242 (Plate 109), 1.9 metres (74.8 in). The frieze tiles may be anything from 24 × 26 cm (9.4 × 10.2 in), and even smaller for those without cornices, to 55 × 40 cm (21.6 × 15.7 in); in general, the larger pieces are of finer quality. The star tiles generally measure between 18 and 24 cm (7.1 and 9.4 in) point to point, though those in the monumental style are smaller (Colour Plate J), and a number of particularly fine pieces in the pre-Mongol period (Plates 106–8) and the 'Veramin' group of 660/1262 (Colour Plate K) are larger, measuring between 28 and 31 cm (11 and 12.2 in).

An examination of the tiles reveals what a small proportion of the production survives. Nine large mihrabs survive (though only sections of two), whose date, potter and provenance are known, while some eighteen dispersed sections of large mihrabs—large pentagonal panels, spandrel tiles and the like—are known without provenance or date. We possess some dozens of individual pieces of frieze tiles, and a greater number of star tiles, which once must have formed part of large groups, but which are now known to us only in solitary examples. On this basis, to make general observations on the level of production at any one time is very risky, and all such comments are put forward here with due reserve.

THE PRE-MONGOL PERIOD

It appears that tiles were not produced in any quantity before about 1200 and the development of the Kashan style of decoration. Tiles decorated in one of the earlier styles are comparatively rare, especially pieces larger than a small star tile, and they differ sharply from the Kashan style pieces in both technical quality and sophistication of painting. The most common type is a small star tile, measuring 13 to 14 cm (5.1 to 5.5 in), and invariably decorated with a seated figure or animal in the monumental style, and with no inscription border (Colour Plate J). Larger pieces include a number of decorative plaques, in both monumental and miniature styles, the most interesting of which (in monumental style) show scenes from the *Shahnama*. The best preserved of the three tiles which survive from this series shows Rustam lifting the rock from the entrance to the cave in which Bizhan had been imprisoned (Plate 102).[2] The figures stand on the base line, and the background is filled with palmette scrolling. The only attempt at a landscape setting is the brick-built structure representing the cave. The inscription above reads 'The coming of Rustam to the head of the pit'. The tile is one of the earliest surviving illustrations from

---

[2]Grube (1976, no. 182). Two other pieces from the same frieze are preserved in Cairo, see Mustafa (1961, no. 38), and in the Iran Bastan Museum, Tehran, no. 4207, unpublished except in Watson (1977, p. 45, fig. 3).

the Persian national epic, and is of a period from which virtually no manuscript or other painted sources survive.[3] A tile in the Berlin-Dahlem Museum with a moulded pointed arch framing is decorated in arabesques of the monumental type, and may once have formed part of a small two-tiled mihrab. It has no inscription.[4]

The development of large-scale decoration with lustre tiles, and the formation of the classic style which was followed by lustre potters for the succeeding century and a half seems to be the creation of two men working in conjunction—Muhammad ibn Abi Tahir and Abu Zaid. The former is the first member of the potting family that dominated production at Kashan, and the latter the man who, as we have seen, may have been largely responsible for the creation of the Kashan style, and was certainly one of its most skilled practitioners.[5] These two potters together worked on the most important of the projects of the pre-Mongol period—the decoration of the tomb-chambers at the shrines at Qumm and Mashhad.

At Qumm the major part of the decoration consisted of a large panel of fifteen tiles signed by Muhammad which covered the top of the sarcophagus (Plate 103). The narrow inscription bands, the very fine detail and rather flat modelling distinguish this piece from the later large mihrabs and show its somewhat experimental style. The sides of the sarcophagus are clad in star and octagonal tiles separated by small double pentagons as at Mashhad (Plate 105) and are also painted in a very similar style with radiating arabesque designs. They all have inscription borders and use blue as well as lustre in the design. Round the top and bottom of the sarcophagus, framing the star tiles, runs an inscription frieze, unusual in that it has no cornice but is flanked top and bottom by a smaller inscription frieze. The main frieze, moulded and in blue against a ground of reserved palmettes, has a Quranic quotation and the signature of Abu Zaid, with the date Rajab 602/February 1206. One of the moulded pilasters that frame the corners of the sarcophagus bears the signature of Muhammad's son Ali, and must be part of a later addition to the decoration of the tomb.[6]

In 612/1215 Muhammad ibn Abi Tahir and Abu Zaid worked on a much more ambitious decoration at Mashhad. The walls of the tomb-chamber were clad in star and octagonal tiles surmounted by a large and impressive inscription frieze (Plate 105), the doorway into the chamber was framed in tiles, and two large mihrabs were installed (Plate 104a, b). It is possible that other areas of the shrine also had dados of lustre tiles. Muhammad was responsible for the

---

[3]An exception is an enamelled beaker in the Freer Gallery of Art, which shows in comic strip form a complete story from the *Shahnama*, see Washington (1973, no. 44); other enamelled bowls show single scenes, see for example, Grube (1976, p. 199 ff).

[4]Sarre (1910, fig. 30) and Berlin (1971, no. 398).

[5]Work by potters mentioned here may be found listed on page 176 ff., and buildings containing tiles on page 183 ff. More information on dated pieces is found in the list on page 189 ff.

[6]Tabataba'i (1976, pp. 46–50, pls. 2–12).

102   TILE. Monumental style, 30.4 × 30.2 cm (11.9 × 11.8 in)
       Keir Collection. See page 123
103   TOMBSTONE PANEL, from the shrine at Qumm. By MUHAMMAD IBN ABI TAHIR,
       datable 602/1206, 290 × 120 cm (114.2 × 47.3 in)
       Shrine Museum, Qumm. See pages 124, 179 and 184

104a   MIHRAB, from the shrine at Mashhad. By ABU ZAID, dated Rabi' II 612/July
1215, height 240 cm (94.5 in) width 184 cm (72.5 in)
In situ, *Mashhad. See pages 122, 124, 126, 180, 185 and 190*

framing round the entrance (and perhaps also for the unsigned mihrab and the
dado frieze tiles), while Abu Zaid's name occurs on one mihrab (Plate 104a, b)
and on a number of the star and octagonal tiles.[7] The quality of this work is
extremely high, with elaborate moulded decoration and very fine detailed
background painting.

   These two schemes at Mashhad and Qumm were not the only large-scale
works undertaken, for fragments of high-quality pieces survive that must once
have belonged to similar ambitious schemes. Muhammad's signature is found
on a fragment of a large mihrab, while an unsigned portion of an inscription

[7]Bahrami (1946a, pp. 37–9, pls. 18–21).

104b Detail of 104a

frieze in the Victoria and Albert Museum, reported to have come from
Mashhad, has finely detailed modelling and painted decoration of an even
higher order than that from the Mashhad shrine.[8]

Abu Zaid's signature is found on a number of star tiles, dated in the first
decade of the century, with painting that must be ranked among the best of the
Kashan potters' production (Plates 106 and 107). On the basis of the signed
pieces one is tempted to ascribe to the same potter a number of other unsigned
stars of similar quality (e.g. Plate 108).[9] These pieces present something of a

[8]Lane (1960, pl. 2a).
[9]See Grube (1961) and Watson (1977, p. 51 ff.) for examples.

105   DADO TILES, from the shrine at Mashhad. Stars signed by ABU ZAID,
       dated 612/1215, height (large frieze tiles) *c*.45 cm (17.7 in)
       In situ, *Mashhad. See pages 28, 122, 124, 146, 180, 185 and 190*

problem, for they are not, as one might have expected, part of the same
decorative scheme, but are dated over a number of years from 600/1203 to
617/1220. The finest pieces have figural decoration and inscriptions of Persian
verses; some even appear to be scenes from the *Shahnama* or other literary
work,[10] though most have the conventional seated figures. They differ from

[10]For example, the tile illustrated by Bahrami (1936, pl. LXVIa) shows a man drawing back his
fist to strike at something held by his other hand (the missing part of the tile is restored with a
fragment from another similar tile). This is very similar to the pose found universally in later
book illustrations of the *Shahnama* scene 'Khusrau and the Lion', see for example L. Binyon,
J. V. S. Wilkinson and B. Gray, *Persian Miniature Painting*, Oxford, 1933, pls. XXXIIc and
LIa.

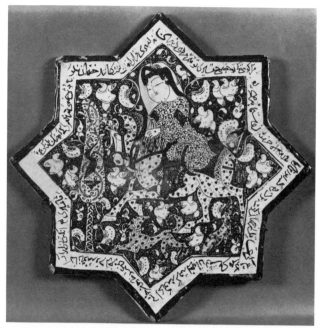

106   STAR TILE. By ABU ZAID, dated Rabi' II 608/September 1211, diameter 28.5 cm
       (11.2 in)
       Museum of Fine Arts, Boston, Ross Collection, 07.903. See pages 123, 127, 180 and 190
107   STAR TILE. By ABU ZAID, dated 607/1210, diameter 28.5 cm (11.2 in)
       Museum of Fine Arts, Boston, Ross Collection, 07.670. See pages 123, 127, 180 and 189

108   STAR TILE. Dated Sha'ban 604/February 1208, diameter 32 cm (12.6 in)
       Museum of Fine Arts, Boston, Ross Collection, 11.40. See pages 123, 127 and 189

the tiles with arabesque and geometric decoration such as those from Mashhad
and Qumm in that they are larger in size (*c.* 28 to 33 cm (11 to 13 in) as opposed
to 22 cm (8.6 in) for the Mashhad stars), and use no blue in the design. That
these tiles appear as singletons may indicate that they were not used in
extensive panels of similar pieces but perhaps as the occasional highlight of a
panel of plain monochrome-glazed tiles.

The star tiles, together with the large mihrabs from Qumm and Mashhad
represent the peak of artistic and technical achievement of the Kashan lustre
potters. The balance between the calligraphy and the background decoration
in the inscription friezes, the elaborate yet lively and uncluttered arabesque
moulding of the mihrabs, and the crisp and sensitive painting of the figures in
the star tiles—all these set standards which were not attained later. The first
wave of Mongol invaders who reached the western Persian provinces in 1220 is
marked by a sudden decline in the quality of the potters' work. It may be unfair

A JAR. Monumental style, height 34 cm (13.4 in)
   Godman Collection, British Museum. See pages 48 and 67

B DISH. Monumental style, diameter 47.3 cm (18.6 in)
Ashmolean Museum, Oxford, 1956–183. See pages 46, 48 and 52

C   JUG. Miniature style, height 17.5 cm (6.9 in)
Victoria and Albert Museum, Clement Ades Gift, no. C167–1977.
See pages 68 and 69

D   DISH. Transitional monumental style, diameter 37 cm (14.5 in)
Ades Family Collection. See pages 28 and 86

E   DISH. Kashan style, dated 604/1207, diameter 35 cm (13.8 in)
   Victoria and Albert Museum, C51–1952. See pages 90, 98, 104, 108, 109 and 198

F   BOWL. Kashan style, by MUHAMMAD IBN ABI AL-HASAN, dated 608/1211,
    diameter 20.4 cm (8 in)
    Iran Bastan Museum, Tehran, 8224. See pages 90, 98, 104, 108, 181 and 198

G   BOWL. Kashan style, by MUHAMMAD IBN MUHAMMAD AL-NISHAPURI, diameter
22.5 cm (8.8 in)
*Victoria and Albert Museum, Clement Ades Gift, C162–1977. See page 41, 43, 93,
98, 104, 108 and 181*

H   BOWL. Il-Khanid period, diameter 21.5 cm (8.4 in)
*Victoria and Albert Museum, C1955–1910. See pages 110 and 111, and Plate 88
for profile*

I   FIGURE OF A LION. Monumental style, height 13.5 cm (5.3 in)
Ades Family Collection. See pages 117 and 118

J   TILE. Monumental style, diameter 13.5 cm (5.3 in)
    Victoria and Albert Museum, C444–1911. See pages 35 and 123

K PANEL OF STARS, from the Imamzada Yahya at Veramin. Dated Dhu'l-Hijja 660 to Safar 661/October to December 1262, diameter (each tile) 31 cm (12.2 in) *Victoria and Albert Museum, 1837–1876. See pages 122, 123, 132, 134, 186 and 191*

M   STAR TILE. Il-Khanid period, diameter 20.5 cm (8 in)
    Victoria and Albert Museum, 1893–1897. See pages 122 and 146

L   *a.* FRIEZE TILE, showing Bahram Gur and Azada, from the Takht-i Sulaiman.
    Datable AD 1270–1275, height 31.5 cm (12.4 in), width 32.3 cm (12.7 in)
    *Victoria and Albert Museum, 1841–1876. Stolen from the Museum in February
    1984. See pages 122, 136, 188, 192*

    b. FRIEZE TILE. Datable AD 1270–1275, height 35.7 cm (14 in), width 36.5 cm
    (14.3 in)
    Victoria and Albert Museum, 541–1900. See page 136

N MIHRAB. Il-Khanid period, pair to that in Plate 125, height 62 cm (24.4 in), width 42 cm (16.5 in)
Victoria and Albert Museum, the 'Salting' mihrab, C1977–1910. See pages 122, 149, and 179

O   BOTTLE. Safavid period, height 26.7 cm (10.5 in).
The photograph shows the full effect of highlights on the uniform lustre pigment
Victoria and Albert Museum, C59–1952. See pages 31 and 165

P SPITTOONS and BOWL. Safavid period, height (bowl) 13 cm (5.1 in)
   Victoria and Albert Museum, 534–1878, 557–1889 and 559–1889. See page 165

to blame the Mongols entirely, for the death or retirement of Muhammad ibn Abi Tahir (last dated work 612/1215) and Abu Zaid (last dated work 616/1219) deprived Kashan of its leading potters and may well have created a vacuum difficult to fill. Certainly al-Hasan ibn Arabshah, whose large mihrab from the Maidan Mosque in Kashan dated 623/1226 is the next recorded major undertaking, is more timid than his predecessors. Though larger than those at Mashhad and Qumm it is simpler in design, with a less complicated system of diminishing niches. The moulded arabesques, though elegant, appear restrained and virtually two dimensional beside those of Abu Zaid. The calligraphy is less striking, and the background decoration less detailed. This is more to praise the painstaking detail and strong sense of design shown by his predecessors than to depreciate the achievement of al-Hasan, which was still considerable, and required extensive workshop resources and design skill. The less exciting impact of his works perhaps reflects the fact that it is by now a 'standard product' of the Kashan potteries, rather than—as twenty years previously—a new venture. Al-Hasan is known for only one other signed work—a pair of frieze tiles in the Victoria and Albert Museum. These may possibly have come from the same scheme as his large mihrab.

IL-KHANID TILES

The 620s/1220s saw a steep decline in the quantity and quality of work produced. Apart from al-Hasan's mihrab only four dated tiles of indifferent quality are known, and only a single piece comes from the next decade (631/1233). Production seems to have picked up in the 650s/1250s, when at least two dated pieces are known, one of them a section of a large or medium mihrab; and in the 660s/1260s production on a large scale was resumed again.

In the midst of this rather depressed period one piece stands out by its ambition, and shows that the potters had not totally given up the idea of grandiose decorative schemes. Originally standing in one of the passages that led into the tomb-chamber at Mashhad, but now removed to the Shrine Museum, is a large mihrab, dated 640/1242 and signed by Muhammad ibn Abi Tahir's son Ali (Plate 109). Smaller than the previous large mihrabs, and simpler in design than even that of al-Hasan ibn Arabshah, it nevertheless attempts to copy the bold and vigorous moulding of his father's work. He is not, at this stage in his career, as skilled, for the cobalt blue that highlighted some of the moulding has run badly. Ali ibn Muhammad, probably within a few years, made another large mihrab, fragments of which have been found in a tomb-tower in the ruins of the old city of Gurgan. He appears to have used the same mould as that in the mihrab of 640/1242 for the tile bearing his signature, though other sections are not the same. It is not, however, until the 660s/1260s that Ali ibn Muhammad's real talents are revealed. In this decade many new commissions were undertaken by the Kashan potters, and his work

109 MIHRAB, from the shrine at Mashhad. By ALI IBN MUHAMMAD IBN ABI TAHIR,
     dated 640/1242, 190 × 125 cm (74.8 × 49.2 in)
     Shrine Museum, Mashhad. See pages 123, 131, 179, 185 and 191

now dominates. The major surviving piece is the large mihrab from the
Imamzada Yahya in Veramin. This formed part of a series of lustre tile
decorations which were installed in the building. The first was a series of
lustred stars and crosses (Colour Plate K) which are dated in the three months
Dhu'l-Hijja 660 to Safar 661/October to December 1262, and were set in dado
panels. Over two years later in Sha'ban 663/May 1265 Ali made his large
mihrab for the same building. The decorations were not completed until some
forty years later when Ali's son Yusuf, together with his partner Ali ibn
Ahmad, made a medium mihrab dated Muharram 705/July 1305, which was
perhaps set on top of the sarcophagus. Unusually, the dado tiles were surmounted not by a tiled frieze but by one of carved plaster dated 707/1307.

110   PANEL OF STAR AND CROSS TILES, from the Imamzada Ja'far at Damghan.
       Dated 664–665/1266–1267, height 80 cm (31.2 in)
       Louvre, 6319. See pages 122, 134, 155, 186 and 191

A number of other commissions can be identified in the 660s/1260s. The Imamzada Ja'far in Damghan was decorated with star and cross tiles, decorated with animal and figure designs, and inscribed with Persian poetry (Plate 110). Dates range from Dhu'l-Hijja 664 to Ramadan 665/September 1266 to May 1267. These tiles, which are smaller, *c.* 21 cm (8.2 in), and use blue and turquoise in their designs, provide a model for most of the stars produced after this date. The figure drawing, as in the vessels, is naive compared to that of the pre-Mongol period but is of great charm and the technical quality is excellent. In 665/1266 a group of star tiles was installed in the Imamzada Ja'far in Qumm, where several broken tiles remain on the sarcophagus, though a number of whole pieces have survived in Western collections. The shrine at Najaf, in present-day Iraq, received a large mihrab, which by comparison with that from the Imamzada Yahya in Veramin can be dated in the 1260s and attributed to Ali ibn Muhammad ibn Abi Tahir. A single tile in the Victoria and Albert Museum from a large or medium mihrab is dated 665/1266 (Plate 111) and may have been part of the decorations already mentioned.

Other pieces dated in this decade are without provenance or companions, but they indicate, together with the known groups, the tremendous surge of activity of the Kashan kilns after a long period of stagnation. Ali ibn Muhammad ibn Abi Tahir is the only potter in this period who signs his work. Both the major schemes, Veramin and Najaf, can be attributed to him and he was responsible no doubt for much else beside. Quality of design and drawing in this period remains high, with great clarity and liveliness (Plates 110 and 111, Colour Plate K), and the technical quality is generally excellent. While not of the sophistication of the best of the pre-Mongol wares, there is still plenty of life and energy at the potters' disposal.

In the following decade the only major commission that can be identified is the decoration for the Mongol sultan Abaqa Khan at his palace on the Takht-i Sulaiman, a natural fortress that rises from the plain in north-west Persia. It had been an important site in the Sasanian period and at times during the Islamic period, perhaps because of its naturally warm lake. Abaqa Khan built an extensive complex there, sections of which were lavishly decorated with tiles in different techniques, including *lajvardina* and lustre. For our purposes the site is of great importance, for it is the sole surviving secular building of the period with lustre decoration. The exact position of many pieces is not certain, for the building has been systematically plundered for years, perhaps centuries (one find during the German Institute's excavations was a hoard of tiles, evidently gathered from various parts of the ruins and set on one side). Lustre star and cross tiles with animal and arabesque decoration were apparently used inside the two kiosks that flanked the main Ivan. These have inscriptions of Persian verse and some are dated in the years 670, 671 and 674/1271, 1272 and 1275. Some have no inscription borders at all. Fragments of pictorial frieze tiles were found elsewhere on the site. These showed scenes of hunting and fighting, and in two cases illustrations of episodes in the *Shahnama* epic:

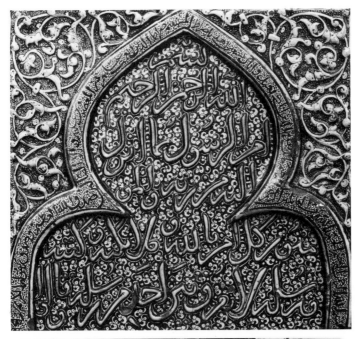

111   TILE. Dated 665/1266, height 52 cm (20.4 in), width 57 cm (22.4 in)
Victoria and Albert Museum, 469–1888. See pages 134 and 191

112   FRIEZE TILE, from the Takht-i Sulaiman. Datable AD 1270–1275, height 30 cm
(11.8 in)
Bargello Museum, 1969. See pages 122, 136, 188 and 192

Faridun riding a cow, and Bahram Gur hunting with his favourite Azada (Colour Plate L), whose disparaging comments on his prowess as an archer led to her being trampled underfoot. Other frieze tiles bear texts from the *Shahnama* in lobed inscription bands, while animal grotesques writhe in the spandrels (Plate 112). It is at Takht-i Sulaiman that are first recorded designs taken direct from Chinese sources, in all probability from textiles. A phoenix and a dragon are found, not in the lustre technique, but in the overglaze gilt and enamel *lajvardina* technique. However, lustred tiles from the same moulds are known, and they must date from the same period or shortly afterwards (Colour Plate La)

Other star tiles, dated variously in the 670s/1270s but without provenance or associated groups, show a steady level of activity at the kilns. One small mihrab is dated 675/1276, but the dating of one medium mihrab is a puzzle (Plate 113). Made up of two tiles, it bears three different dates: Muharram 670/August 1271, Safar 670/September 1271 and, in numerals 667/1268! The inscriptions, which are entirely Quranic, offer no explanation. This mihrab was removed from the top of the sarcophagus of Habib ibn Musa, in Kashan. The sides of the sarcophagus contain an inscription frieze and a number of stars and crosses (Plate 114) which are of interest because they have figural and animal decoration, the only such pieces remaining *in situ* in a religious building.

More dated star tiles survive from the 680s/1280s than from the previous decade, but only one complex can be identified—the decoration of the tomb-chamber of the Pir-i Husain mausoleum in Baku. Here star tiles with inscription friezes were used as dado panels on the walls and to clad the sides of the sarcophagus, which had a coffin-shaped element built up of specially shaped tiles on its top. The star tiles range in date from 681 to 684/1282 to 1285, which latter date occurs also on the frieze. The painting of these tiles is less good than that found on tiles twenty years previously. The arabesque and geometric designs have a scrappy and monotonous quality. The lower tile of a medium mihrab dated 688/1289, and a small mihrab dated 689/1290, are the only other signs of special commissions.

The 690s/1290s appear to have been a depressed decade for the potteries. A mere five dated stars are known, and no more ambitious pieces. The first decade of the next century sees an upturn in production again. In Rabi' I 700/November 1300 some two hundred and fifty tiles were installed in the mosque of Ali in the village of Quhrud near Kashan (Plate 115). Decorated in arabesque and floral motifs they have Quranic inscriptions, and differ from the general run of stars in that they are six- not eight-pointed.

In Muharram 705/August 1305 we have the first recorded work of Ali ibn Muhammad's son Yusuf, who together with the potter Ali ibn Ahmad ibn Ali al-Husaini made a medium mihrab which was installed in the Imamzada Yahya in Veramin along with his father's work. More important work was done slightly more than two years later in Shawwal 707/March 1308 at the shrine of Abd al-Samad at Natanz. None of the tiling remains *in situ*, but

113 MIHRAB, from the Imamzada Habib ibn Musa in Kashan. Dated 667 and
670/1268–1271, height 133 cm (52.4 in), width 57 cm (22.4 in)
Iran Bastan Museum, Tehran, 3289. See pages 122, 136, 186 and 191

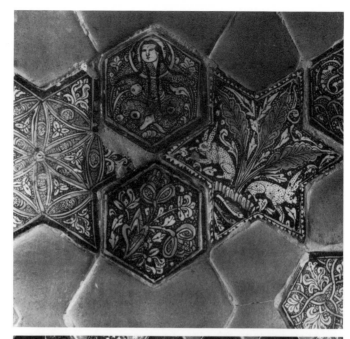

114   TILES, on the sarcophagus of Habib ibn Musa in Kashan. Width (star)
*c.*15 cm (5.9 in)
In situ, *Kashan. See pages 122, 136, 146, 155 and 186*

115   STAR TILES with turquoise hexagons, in the Mosque of Ali, Quhrud. Dated
Rabi' I 700/November 1300 and Rabi' II 707/October 1307, diameter (star)
19 cm (7.5 in)
In situ, *Quhrud. See pages 122, 136, 146, 155, 187 and 194*

116   FRIEZE TILE, from the shrine at Natanz. Dated Shawwal 707/March 1308,
      height 36 cm (14.1 in)
      Victoria and Albert Museum, 1485–1876. See pages 122, 140, 187 and 195
117   SECTION OF MIHRAB, from the shrine at Natanz. Dated 707/1307,
      width 82 cm (32.3 in)
      Victoria and Albert Museum, 71–1885. See pages 140, 187 and 194

records from the last century give us a fairly good indication of what was originally there. A series of frieze tiles, one of which bears the date, with a decoration of birds among foliage in the background to the inscription and on the cornice (which now, through an excess of religious zeal, have all had their heads chipped off), are recorded in the registers of the Musée des Arts Décoratifs in Paris as having come from the 'Medresse (Collège) de Nûtens, entre Téhéran et Ispahàn' (Plate 116). The Victoria and Albert Museum possesses an extraordinary niche-head which, uniquely among lustre tile constructions, is of three dimensional form, with the curved niche recessing some 15 cm (5.9 in). It is recorded as coming from 'a ruined shrine or mosque at Natenz' and has an inscription which also ends in the date 707/1307 (Plate 117). The same museum also possesses a number of pieces of small inscription frieze, without cornices, but some with moulded fillets top and bottom and some plain. These were no doubt incorporated into some complex structure with the niche. The walls of the shrine were covered with stars and crosses, but as none remain *in situ* and museum records do not attribute any to this site we cannot be sure exactly which they were. As other pieces from the shrine have entered Western collections it is reasonable to assume that a number of the stars have as well, and on the basis of one dated piece, one may suggest a group with arabesque and other decoration, and inscriptions in reserve, as a possible candidate.

In the same year, 707/1307, the mosque of Ali in Quhrud had a further group of tiles added to its decoration of seven years previously. Identical in shape and similar in design, they differ in having inscriptions in Persian verse rather than quotations from the Quran.

Eight sections from an inscription frieze dated Sha'ban 709/January 1310 are preserved, one of which bears the signature of Yusuf ibn Ali ibn Muhammad ibn Abi Tahir. It is remarkable for its high technical quality and clean drawing. The same qualities and similar treatment of the foliage background are seen in a large frieze without cornice from the Godman Collection (Plate 118), and in a smaller frieze of similar design.[11] Unfortunately we have no other pieces we can associate with these, nor any indication of provenance. From the next decade we have another set of frieze tiles, of which only those bearing the date Ramadan 710/January 1311 and the signature of Yusuf ibn Ali ibn Muhammad survive. Dated in the same year is a medium mihrab which records the erection of a number of mihrabs and inscriptions in an unspecified building. Another medium mihrab is dated Rabi' II 713/July 1313 and is possibly signed by Ali ibn Ahmad. Stars are dated 710 (Plate 119), 711 and two 713/1310–1313; but from the latter part of the decade only one dated star of 717/1317 is recorded, and a frieze dated Rajab 718/August 1318 from the Imamzada Ali ibn Ja'far in Qumm.

[11]London (1976, nos. 376–7).

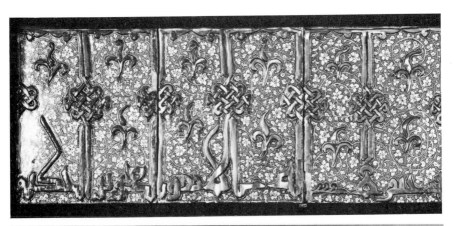

118   FRIEZE TILES. Height 57 cm (22.4 in), width 141 cm (55.5 in)
       Godman Collection, British Museum. See page 140

119   STAR TILE. Dated 710/1310, diameter 20.5 cm (8 in)
       Museum of Fine Arts, Boston, 31.729. See pages 140 and 195

The following decade is represented by only three dated stars, and after this depressed performance, it is perhaps rather surprising to see what appears to be a burst of activity in the 730s/1330s. In Ramadan 734/May 1334 Yusuf ibn Ali ibn Muhammad ibn Abi Tahir made his only recorded large mihrab for the Imamzada Ali ibn Ja'far in Qumm (Plate 120). Larger than any of the other mihrabs, it fails to match them in other respects. The moulded decoration is somewhat clumsy, the painting hurried and simplified, and the technical quality of the lustre not of the highest order. Better in both quality of painting and technique are a series of stars installed in the same building and dated from Rabi' I to Jumada I 738/October to December 1337 (Plate 121). Two pieces record the names of the artist and the workshop owner: '. . . in the place Kashan in the workshop of Sayyid of Sayyids, Sayyid Rukn al-Din Muhammad son of the late Sayyid Zain al-Din Ali, the potter; the work of the most noble, the most excellent master, Master Jamal, the painter (al-naqqash)'. One would not ascribe to the same workshop the two other groups of tiles made in the same year which show ponderous or careless painting. One group, still in situ in the shrine of Muhammad al-Hanafiyya on the island of Kharg, is decorated with foliage, birds or geometric motifs in a stiff and clumsy hand. The second group, dated between Rabi' I and Jumada II 738/October 1337 to January 1338, are drawn in a scrappy and careless manner. Of somewhat better quality is a series of frieze tiles dated Dhu' l-Hijja 738/June 1338. Probably to roughly the same date is to be assigned the medium mihrab by Ahmad ibn Ali al-banna, 'the builder', whose work in stucco is also known (Plate 126).[12]

This activity would seem to bode well for the Kashan kilns, but fate was not to be kind. Four stars are dated 739/1338, evidently related to the scrappily painted group mentioned above. One of these, decorated with a seated figure partaking of a bowl of fruit and an attendant proffering a wine bottle, bears the slightly desperate plea at the end of the inscription '. . . in the place Kashan, may Allah, be He exalted, protect it from the accidents of time' (Plate 122). This cry for help (in the face of declining orders?) went unheeded, however, for one single star tile dated 740/1339 marks the end of the sequence of lustre tiling that had been produced for some 140 years, lapsing only during and after the Mongol invasions.

The above account is based on the major dated groups. There are, however, a number of pieces of interest that cannot be grouped nor assigned provenance or dates with any degree of accuracy. A large number of star tiles was made which instead of a painted inscription border have an inscription or geometric design reserved in white on a blue ground. The blue tends to flow, so lustre is used to outline the letters precisely. Dated pieces range in this group from 665 to 729/1226 to 1328. Many of the designs are floral or arabesque, but animals

---

[12]See page 180, note 9.

120   MIHRAB, from the Imamzada Ali ibn Ja'far, Qumm. By YUSUF IBN ALI
      MUHAMMAD IBN ABI TAHIR, dated 734/1334, height 328 cm (129.2 in), width
      212 cm (83.5 in)
      *Iran Bastan Museum, Tehran, 3270. See pages 122, 123, 142, 179, 184–5, 195
      and 196*

121   PANEL OF STARS, from the Imamzada Ali ibn Ja'far, Qumm. By MASTER JAMAL in
      the workshop of RUKN AL-DIN MUHAMMAD, dated Rabi' I to Jumada I 738/October
      to December 1337, diameter (each star) 23.4 cm (9.2 in)
      Iran Bastan Museum, Tehran, 4481. See pages 122, 142, 181, 184 and 196
122   STAR TILE. Dated 739/1338, diameter 23 cm (9 in)
      British Museum, OA+ 1123. See pages 142 and 196

123 STAR TILE. Il-Khanid period, diameter 20.5 cm (8 in)
Walters Art Gallery, Baltimore, 48.1288. See pages 146 and 153

124 TILE, from the shrine of the 'Footprint of Ali', Kashan. Bearing the date Shawwal
711/ February 1312, diameter 28.5 cm (11.2 in)
Musée de Sèvres, Paris, 22688. See pages 146, 186 and 195

and human figures are also common; a number of moulded designs are known, with floral designs or flying birds (Colour Plate M). A few show quite exceptional scenes: a couple kissing,[13] a couple in bed, with an attendant at the door,[14] and two men engaged in an undignified brawl (Plate 123). These may be intended as illustrations to epic stories, though the text of the last tile describes the great hero Rustam preparing himself for hunting, and bears no relation to the image.

Another distinct group follows the designs of the standard types of tile, but is much smaller; some of these have completely illegible inscriptions.

Stars of odd shapes indicate that the eight-pointed star and cross pattern was not the only system in use. The stars and octagons separated by double pentagons have already been seen at Mashhad (Plate 105), as has the six-pointed star with hexagons at Kashan and Quhrud (Plates 114 and 115). A six-pointed star in the Musée des Arts Décoratifs in Paris evidently alternated with octagons, and a small polygonal tile with a vertical axis and somewhat spearheaded form in the Victoria and Albert Museum must have formed part of a very complicated geometric pattern.[15]

A unique piece is preserved in the Museum of Sèvres. Circular in shape, with a raised border that does not quite run all the way round (Plate 124), the tile is a foundation plaque and the long text tells the story of the circumstances surrounding the foundation of a shrine,[16] and explains the curious shape of the tile. It reveals that on the dawn of Thursday 10 February 1312 (1 Shawwal 711) a certain Sayyid Fakhr al-Din Hasan Tabari dreamt that he was in a garden just outside one of Kashan's gateways, and saw there a large group of people standing round a tent, outside which were tethered a horse and a camel. A beautiful young man, dressed in Arab clothes, invited him into the tent, where was sitting an awe-inspiring warrior whose 'bravery and majesty made the earth to move and the light from whose blessed face reached the sky'. This was Ali, the Prophet's son-in-law and the first Imam of the Shi'i sect, who indicated that he was going to India to convert the heathen. He wished for a magnificent chapel to be built as a place of pilgrimage for those not able to travel to India. The dreamer then awoke, and going to the garden, marked the place where the Imam had been sitting, and discovered footprints of the horse and camel. The Imam later appeared to a number of other people, and commanded that a certain Haidar Faris should undertake to construct the monument, which he then did. The inscription at the sides of the raised border reads: 'He saw in the day a horse-shoe of this size', the border representing the size of the footprint of the Imam's horse.[17] The founding of such a building

---

[13]Watson (1977, p. 85, fig. 84), in the Musée de Sèvres, otherwise unpublished.

[14]Wolfe (1975, no. 122); present whereabouts unknown.

[15]Nos. (Arts Décoratifs) 17456 and (Victoria and Albert Museum) 923–1898; Watson (1977, figs. 6–7) otherwise unpublished.

[16]The full text is given by Adle (1972).

[17]Chahryar Adle has recently discovered an old photograph showing this tile with a now missing companion tile, whose shape is based on an imprint of the camel's hoof, and which is decorated with a picture of tent, horse and camel. See Adle (1982).

125   MIHRAB. By ALI IBN AHMAD IBN ALI AL-HUSAINI, pair to Colour Plate N,
height 62 cm (24.4 in), width 46 cm (18.1 in)
Victoria and Albert Museum, 1527–1876. See pages 122, 149 and 179

126 MIHRAB. By HASAN IBN ALI IBN AHMAD, height 123.2 cm (48.5 in)
*Metropolitan Museum of Art, New York, 09.87. See pages 122, 142
and 180*

after the vision of the Imam is not a unique occurrence, for a similar story is told of the founding of the mosque of Ali in Quhrud just outside Kashan. In this case the details are not told on the lustre tiles installed in the mosque, but on a fine carved wooden door.[18]

The occurrence of mihrab tiles in pairs is worthy of note. The potter Ali ibn Ahmad ibn Ali al-Husaini was mentioned above when he signed a medium mihrab with Yusuf of the Abu Tahir family. A pair of small mihrabs may also be assigned to him, on the basis of his signature which occurs on one of them: 'the weak slave in need of the mercy of Allah, be He exalted, Ali ibn Ahmad ibn Ali ibn Abi Al-Husain wrote (decorated) this in his own hand in the months (of the year) . . .'. There was not, unfortunately, sufficient room to include the date (Plate 125). The pair to it is unsigned, but follows the design exactly (Colour Plate N).[19] It was not taken from the same mould, as it bears different inscriptions and different arabesque mouldings. Another pair of small mihrabs were taken from a single mould, and bear the date 668/1269; while yet another pair, undated, show by different inscriptions and arabesque mouldings that they were taken from different moulds.[20] One might suggest, by analogy with the pairs of tombstones that occur in the fifteenth century (see page 160), that these pieces also are tombstones and were designed to be set at either side or on either end of a sarcophagus, rather than as directional niches. Similar designs occur on carved stone tombstones of the same period.

[18] Watson (1975a, pp. 69–70).
[19] Lane (1960, pl. 1a).
[20] In the Gulbenkian Museum, Lisbon; see Gulbenkian (1963, no. 18). Its pair is in the Musée des Arts Décoratifs, Paris, no. 7643a.

Chapter 11

IMAGES, INSCRIPTIONS AND THE USE OF LUSTRE TILES

IMAGES AND INSCRIPTIONS

The bulk of inscriptions found on lustre ware of the pre-Mongol and Il-Khanid periods fall into two categories: Quranic quotations and 'secular' verse. The Quranic quotations occur only on tiles; verse, however, appears on both tiles and vessels. The Quranic quotations on tiles are taken from a limited selection—the whole text of the Quran is by no means found—and certain favoured passages predominate. On star tiles, for example, the first and the hundred-and-twelfth suras are frequently combined:

(Sura 1)

      In the Name of God, the Merciful, the Compassionate

      Praise belongs to God, the Lord of all Being
      the All-merciful, the All-compassionate,
      the Master of the Day of Doom.
      Thee only we serve; to Thee alone we pray for succour,
      Guide us in the straight path,
      the path of those whom Thou hast blessed,
      not of those against whom Thou art wrathful,
      nor of those who are astray.

(Sura 112)

      In the Name of God, the Merciful, the Compassionate

      Say: 'He is God One,
      God, the Everlasting Refuge,
      who has not begotten, and has not been begotten,
      and equal to Him is not any one.'

The Throne Verse (sura 2, v. 255) is another passage found frequently on both mihrabs and star tiles:

> God
> there is no god but He, the
> Living, the Everlasting.
> Slumber seizes Him not, neither sleep;
> to Him belongs
> all that is in the heavens and the earth.
> Who is there that shall intercede with Him
> save by His Leave?
> He knows what lies before them
> and what is after them,
> and they comprehend not anything of His knowledge
> save such as He wills,
> His Throne comprises the heavens and earth;
> the preserving of them oppresses Him not;
> He is the All-high, the All-glorious.

For the rest there is some indication that the choice of passage was not entirely arbitrary. Tiles known to have come from tombs are mostly inscribed with suras from the latter part of the Quran—suras which in large part deal with the Day of Judgement and the horrors of hell, while those from the mosque at Quhrud, for example, are taken from the central portions of the Quran which stress man's duty to God during his life.[1] Each selection appears suited to the type of building the tiles adorned. As telling, though puzzling, is the absence of the Verse of Light (sura 24, v. 35), which compares the Light of Allah to a lamp in a niche. This is not found on mihrab tiles where moulded decoration of hanging lamps make clear reference to it, and this must be a deliberate omission.[2]

The 'secular' verse is of two types—quatrains and passages from epic texts. Some hundred of the quatrains have been read, and they share a common subject matter—the agonies of love—and, in general, a low level of literary accomplishment.[3] While some have been identified as the work of minor contemporary poets, others are evidently the work of the potters themselves—a fact that Abu Zaid for one brings to the reader's attention.[4] The following examples are the commonest that occur, and are typical of the whole group. They occur on vessels and tiles during the whole century and a half of pre-Mongol and Il-Khanid production.

[1] Watson (1975a, pp. 63–7).
[2] Only one example of this verse has been recorded, on a star tile, decorated with a gazelle amidst flowers, see Zander (1914, no. 399).
[3] See in particular Bahrami (1936, 1937 and 1949a), and London (1979, pp. 54–9).
[4] London (1979, p. 11) and Watson (in press (a)).

Oh, satiated men of the world are eager for your kindness,
The heroes of the world are frightened of separation from you.
What have the gazelles on the plain to compare with your eyes?
The lions of the world are caught in your hair.

Oh, you whose will it is to hurt me for years and months,
Who are free from me and glad at my anguish,
You vowed not to break your promise again.
It is I, who have caused this break.

Oh, you who please me, do you know why
My two oppressed eyes are full of tears?
From ardent desire of your lips, my eyes draw forth
Water from the mouth of my pupils.

Epic verse is more commonly found on star tiles, though examples on frieze tiles and even vessels are known. They are again a limited selection, and two passages from Firdausi's *Shahnama* account for the majority of identified examples.[5] The first consists of the opening lines of the epic:

In the name of the Lord of the soul and of wisdom
Than Whom thought can conceive nothing higher,
The Lord of all things nameable and of all space,
The Lord who grants sustenance and is our Guide.

The second from the story of Rustam:

From the Priest we are told the story in this way:
'That at dawn Rustam prepared,
His heart was troubled, he prepared for hunting,
He fastened his belt, his quiver was full of arrows.'

The first quotation, being religious, presents no problem; the second, however, is something of a puzzle, for it does not describe a particularly dramatic or significant moment of the story. The frequency with which these lines are repeated on tiles from a single group with no attempt to continue the text on other tiles suggests that the reason for its choice lay in something other than the quality of the narrative.

To this puzzling observation, we may add another: the lack of relationship in general between image and inscription on both vessels and tiles. While the common image of two figures seated together may possibly be thought suitable as an illustration to some of the 'love' verses (though these usually deal with the tortures of *separation* rather than the pleasures of the loved one's company), we also find such verses together with images of enthroned figures, hunters,

---

[5]See the publications, in Russian, by L. T. Gyuzalyan.

polo players, and animals. These images are often explained as part of a 'princely cycle' and sit ill with the tenor of the verses. Similarly, the description of Rustam preparing for hunting quoted above is found on tiles decorated respectively with two undignified old men brawling (Plate 123), a figure seated under an awning, a single seated figure (none of these people armed or with quivers), a rabbit and two gazelles, as well as on many with non-figurative decoration. None of these images is apt as an illustration of the text. The converse is also seen. A small group of pre-Mongol tiles are decorated with what appear to be illustrations from epic texts: Khusrau killing the lion outside Shirin's tent (lion and tent unfortunately missing and replaced with fragments from another star),[6] and Faridun and Kava are among the more precisely identifiable scenes.[7] Yet the texts on these stars appear to be inappropriate 'love' quatrains. The most useful suggestion for interpreting image and text is that of Oleg Grabar, who argues that their correspondence is not to be found on 'a narrative and illustrative level but on some other level, just as the text and the image of a Christmas card do not necessarily relate to each other, although both reflect . . . sentiments accepted as being appropriate to the occasion'.[8] In order to investigate further the 'occasion' which might reunite such seemingly disparate elements we must turn to the buildings in which the lustre tiles were used.[9]

BUILDINGS

In spite of the fact that large numbers of tiles are no longer in the buildings for which they were made, but have been removed to museum collections, we are able to identify a fair number of buildings from which they came. While these are surely only a fraction of the total number of buildings which were originally decorated with lustre tiles, the consistency of the type of building in which they occur allows us to make some generalizations.

Of the twenty-one securely recorded religious buildings, eighteen are tombs, two are mosques and one is a shrine. The strong funerary association is strengthened upon closer inspection; the one shrine, that of Ali in Kashan, commemorates a vision of the Imam Ali (page 146), and though technically not a tomb, acted as one in that it became a place of veneration and pilgrimage, and the focus of a cemetery that grew up around it. It can thus be classed with the other tombs. The mosque of Ali in Quhrud was built on the order of the same Imam who again appeared in a vision, and though the building functions as a mosque, the inscriptions on its doorway show clearly that it was also regarded

[6]Wiet (1935a, p. 5, no. 9).
[7]Unpublished except in Watson (1977, p. 52, fig. 8).
[8]O. Grabar, 'The Visual Arts', in J. A. Boyle (ed.), *The Cambridge History of Iran*, vol. 5, Cambridge, 1968, p. 647.
[9]A list of buildings is given on pages 184–8.

as a commemorative building. The Maidan Mosque in Kashan, which housed the famous Berlin mihrab, is in fact a fifteenth-century building, and the early thirteenth-century mihrab was re-used. This building should then be disregarded. The funerary association of the tiles is made more plain by their position in some of the larger complexes: In Qumm, Mashhad, Baku and Natanz, it is the tomb-chambers that are decorated with lustre tiles, not the associated mosques or other areas. In addition, four 'mihrabs' without provenance show by their inscriptions that they are tombstones (see page 188), and lustre tiles have in several instances been picked up on the sites of cemeteries.

Perhaps more surprising than the funerary association is that the buildings are almost exclusively those of the minority Shi'ite sect. The Shi'is had been systematically persecuted by the Saljuqs but in the freer more tolerant atmosphere under the Il-Khans they consolidated their position in society, developing in strength and existing as substantial minorities, and on occasion as majorities in towns throughout Persia.[10] Qumm, Najaf and Mashhad were their most important shrines, and Qumm their centre of theological studies. Gurgan, Kashan, where the tiles were all made, and Veramin are known to have been strong Shi'ite centres;[11] the tombs at Damghan and Kharg are of descendants of one or other of the Shi'ite Imams, while at Natanz an inscription on the façade gives the Shi'ite creed 'Ali is the *Wali* of Allah'. A number of tiles of unrecorded provenance bear the same text.[12] Only Baku, Sarvistan and Yazd are not known to have been Shi'ite. However, in Baku and Sarvistan the tiles decorate the tombs of Sufi masters whose names at least show them to have sympathy with the Shi'is.

To this very specific use of the lustre tiles we can add a further surprising observation: tiles with 'secular' decoration were intended to decorate religious monuments. In the past it was deemed self-evident that those tiles with Quranic inscriptions were for use in religious buildings, and those with 'secular' verse for use in palaces, baths and the like. The discovery of tiles with 'secular' inscriptions and decoration in a religious context—at Damghan—was explained by their being the decoration of a ruined palace re-used in the tomb.[13] The necessity of frequent recourse to this story as research progressed

[10]For the development of Shi'ism in Iran in the period in question, see the relevant chapters of *The Cambridge History of Iran*, vol. 5, Cambridge, 1968.
[11]Mustaufi's *Nuzhat al-Qulub*, a geographical account of the Mongol period, gives valuable information on these points, see Mustaufi (1958).
[12]Four medium mihrabs show by the inclusion of the phrase 'Ali is the Friend of Allah' that they were installed in Shi'ite buildings: one dated 663/1269 (page 191); one in the Royal Scottish Museum, 1921–1319 (unpublished); one in the Victoria and Albert Museum, no. 1480–1886, Murdoch Smith (n.d., p. 32); and one on the art market in 1976 (unpublished). See Watson (1977, p. 141). No tiles are known whose inscriptions contain anything indicative of Sunni loyalty, such as blessings on the *Rashidun* caliphs.
[13]The story occurs when the tiles were first described in print by the Persian traveller Sani' al-Daula (1884, III, pp. 273–5) and was repeated by later writers, e.g. Bahrami (1936, p. 187) and Sarre (1910, pp. 67–8).

rendered it more and more doubtful and a different explanation is called for. At present, tiles with 'secular' inscriptions—quatrains or epic verse—have been found in a large number of religious buildings: in Qumm (in the Imamzada Ali ibn Ja'far), in Baku, in Damghan (Plate 110), in Kharg and in Quhrud (Plate 115). The evidence of the Quhrud tiles is of particular importance: a group of 'secular' tiles were made to special order for this mosque matching the unique size and shape of 'religious' tiles installed a few years previously. Similarly in Baku the 'secular' tiles are of the same series as the 'religious' and do not look like later intrusions. At Kharg and at Damghan, only tiles with 'secular' inscriptions are found. Furthermore, at Damghan, Kashan (Plate 114) and Qumm tiles with human figures are found in the religious buildings. It seems then that we must consider a religious interpretation of these 'secular' decorations. It is, of course, the presence of tiles in the two Sufi monuments that provides us with the clue. In their writing, the Sufis make much use of allegory to illustrate their view of the world and the nature of the mystic quest. Their subject matter ranges wide but makes particular use of human love and drunkenness as an image for divine love and spiritual intoxication. Separation from and ill treatment by the loved one—the predominant theme of the quatrains on the tiles—are much beloved allegories to illustrate the mystic's separation from the Godhead. Animals stories are used to illustrate moral truths. Indeed, so far-ranging and flexible is Sufi imagery that all motifs and themes found on lustre tiles are susceptible of a Sufi interpretation. Mystic speculation has been strongly posited as an element in the decoration of other decorative arts of the period,[14] has been convincingly argued in the case of the lustre dish (Plate 63),[15] and must be accepted in the case of the lustre tiles. We know that at the period in question the Sufis were adopting many Shi'ite beliefs, and evidently their own view of the world was also gaining adherents.[16] However, it is at a popular level of religious experience that the decoration and inscriptions are to be understood. In the major shrines, particularly that at Mashhad and that of Fatima at Qumm, which were run by the highest level of trained clergy, we find no departure from accepted 'Islamic' iconography—no animal or figural decoration, no 'secular' verse, just the Quran and Hadith of the Prophet, with foliate patterns or arabesques. It is in the minor shrines, more likely to have been controlled by the local populace, that one finds the mystic and 'unorthodox' decoration.[17] Popular religious practice, which in Persia maintains to this day pre- or un-Islamic superstitions and beliefs, also

[14]A. S. Melikian Chirvani has in his numerous writings continually stressed the esoteric and mystical nature of decoration on Persian metalwork. See especially his *Islamic Metalwork from the Iranian World*, London, HMSO, 1982, p. 16ff and passim.
[15]Ettinghausen (1961).
[16]A. Bausani, 'Religion under the Mongols', *Cambridge History of Iran*, vol. 5, Cambridge, 1968, p. 538 ff.
[17]Orthodox disapproval of figural representation was felt sufficiently strongly by the potters and their clients to ensure that no tile was decorated with human figures and Quranic verse; tiles with animal decoration and Quranic verse, on the other hand, are common.

explains the presence of epic verse on the tiles. There is a text roughly contemporary with the tiles which complains of the use of religious propagandists sent 'to spread idle tales in all the bazaars of the country . . .' who '. . . invented false wars and unfounded stories concerning Rustam, Suhrab, Isfandiyar . . .'.[18] The fact that this is a Shi'i complaining of Sunni practice does not mean that similar use of the histories of pre-Islamic kings did not form part of the religious expression of Shi'ism at a popular level.

In short, the use of lustre tiling is far from being just part of the increased use of tiles in architecture in the thirteenth and fourteenth centuries. They appear to be specific in their use—restricted largely to the decoration of funerary monuments of the minority Shi'i sect. The potters, working in Kashan, were certainly Shi'ite themselves. The apparently 'secular' nature of tile decoration from religious monuments must be explained by religious practice influenced by Sufi thought at a popular level.

What, then, of the secular use of lustre tiles? We cannot deny such use, for tiles were excavated at the Mongol palace at Takht-i Sulaiman. However, we cannot tell, by subject matter of image or inscription alone, whether a piece was designed for a religious building or not. The tiles from Takht-i Sulaiman are indistinguishable in any formal sense from those tiles found in religious monuments.[19] We are lucky that this palace survives even as an archaeological ruin—we have no other domestic buildings of the period—but we cannot say whether this use of lustre tiles was an extraordinary or a common occurrence.[20]

One may at this point even extend the speculation to the lustre vessels, for they are decorated with exactly the same scenes and quatrains as the tiles. Were these then, to the pious Shi'i, also imbued with religious significance? We cannot, in the present state of our knowledge, do more than suggest the possibility.

[18]Qazvini's *Kitab al-Naqd*, quoted in A. Bausani, 'Religion in the Saljuq Period', *Cambridge History of Iran*, vol. 5, Cambridge, 1968, pp. 293–4.

[19]The large frieze tiles with figurative decoration or epic verse have not been found in any religious context, though both are found in religious buildings on star tiles.

[20]Ibn Battuta, travelling through the Middle East in the mid-fourteenth century, reports seeing *Qashani* tiles in six sites, which include the shrines at Najaf and Mashhad, two mosques in Tabriz and Qalhat, a Hamam in Isfahan and a garden waterworks near Smyrna. These have often been taken to be lustre tiles, and the evidence used to demonstrate their widespread use. In fact they are not described in sufficient detail to be identified as lustre tiles, nor is the adjective 'golden' used, which Ibn Battuta uses of the lustre ware of Malaga. The situations in which the *Qashani* are described, mostly covering outside walls, and the comparison with North African *zalij* tiles, tend to suggest that he saw mosaic tilework. The use of the word *Qashani* for tilework in general reflects Kashan's major place in ceramic production, going far beyond lustre ware alone. See *Voyages d'Ibn Batoutah*, ed. C. Defremery and B. Sanguinetti, Paris, 1853–8, i/415, ii/46, 130, 225 and 297, and iii/78–9.

Chapter 12

LATER LUSTRE WARE

Towards the end of the first half of the fourteenth century the stream of lustre ceramics from the Kashan kilns came virtually to a halt. No more were made of the standard star, frieze and mihrab tiles which had been the mainstay of the kilns during the Il-Khanid period. We do not know the reasons for the collapse—whether it was economic, for instance, the lustre potters being unable to compete with the rapidly developing faience mosaic,[1] or social, such tiles no longer being required or fashionable. It may even have been because of the death of the master potters, leaving behind no skilled successors. A few clumsily decorated frieze and star tiles, on clay rather than frit bodies, have been found in the Kirman region, and these may perhaps be the products of a Kashan potter who had sought a new centre after the collapse of his home-town workshops. These tiles were, at any rate, not produced for long.[2] Another batch of stars, of unknown provenance, decorated in a dull lustre pigment, bear a distant relationship to those of Kashan, though a characteristic spiky leaf is an indication of fifteenth-century date (Plate 127). One of these is signed by an otherwise unknown potter Diya al-Din ibn Sayyid Sharaf al-Din Husain al-Husaini. Apart from these odd pieces, it is the existence of a dated bowl and a series of inscription tiles and tombstones, some of which were made for buildings in the Kashan area, that demonstrate to us that the technique was not entirely lost. The dates of these pieces range from 1418 to 1560, and they are evidence of the link between the Il-Khanid wares, and the Safavid production of the seventeenth century.

The bowl is the earliest in date. It shows a bird with outspread wings surrounded by smaller birds and foliage. The inscription band separates this from a broad frieze of small birds and foliage round the rim, and repeats a simple blessing with the date 822/1418.[3] The drawing is highly stylized, but

[1] See D. Wilber, 'The Development of Mosaic Faience in Islamic Architecture in Iran', *Ars Islamica*, VI, 1939.
[2] Watson (1975b, p. 75, pl. VI).
[3] Sold in Paris (1981, lot 70, with illustration).

127 STAR TILES. One signed by DIYA AL-DIN IBN SAYYID SHARAF AL-DIN HUSAIN
     AL-HUSAINI, 15th century, diameter 13 cm (5.1 in)
     *Ashmolean Museum, Oxford. X3167, X3189, X3191, X3194. See pages 157
     and 182*

128 BOTTLE. Late 14th or early 15th century, height 30.4 cm (12 in)
     Godman Collection, British Museum. See page 160

129 BUILDING FOUNDATION TILE. By Nusrat al-Din Muhammad, with the name of
     Sultan Abu Saʿid, dated 860/1455, height 30.4 cm (12 in)
     *Metropolitan Museum of Art, New York, Bequest of Theodore M. Davis, 1915,
     30.95.26. See pages 160, 182 and 197*
130 FRIEZE TILES. From the same building as Plate 126, with part of the titles and
     name of Sultan Abu Saʿid, datable to 860/1455, height 30.5 cm (12 in), width
     31.3 cm (12.3 in)
     Victoria and Albert Museum, C26 + a–1983. See page 160

shows none of the Chinese elements usually found in wares attributed to this date.[4] It represents a degenerate form of the fourteenth-century tradition of lustre painting. A cut-down bottle in the Godman Collection shows a frieze of birds in a similar pose and with details of decoration similar to the bird on the dated bowl (Plate 128).[5] Its more fluent style of painting, however, suggests an earlier date, perhaps towards the end of the fourteenth century. The two pieces together demonstrate that, for a while at least, vessels were also produced, though we cannot tell exactly for how long, in what quantities or where.

A group of tiles record the erection of a building by the Timurid sultan Abu Sa'id in the year 860/1455. Two large tiles, taken from the same mould, show a simple niche enclosing moulded arabesques, with an inscription border. The painted inscription differs slightly on each tile, but both give the name of the sultan and the date; one is signed by Nusrat al-Din Muhammad (Plate 129). Four tiles from a continuous frieze bear the name of the same sultan and part of his titles (Plate 130).[6] All these tiles are closely related in the style of the calligraphy and in their technical characteristics. While not as ambitious as similar pieces from the twelfth and thirteenth centuries, they are competently made. A transparent glaze covers a white granular body and the lustre is of a curious tomato-red colour. The whole group was evidently made for the same, as yet unidentified, building. While the tiles are technically mediocre, the calligraphy is of a high order.

Not even this much can be said of the following pieces, whose crude moulding and indifferent or bad calligraphy mark them out as provincial. The tombstone for the lady Bibi Malik Khatun, dated 886/1481 (Plate 131), and the pair of tombstones for Muhammad, the tailor of Aran, dated 891/1486 (Plate 132) evidently issue from the same workshop, so similar are the crude designs. The next piece, though of better quality, is also probably from the same workshop. It records the donation of some carpets to the shrine of Shah Yalman (situated in the Kashan bazaar) in the year 902/1496, and is signed by the potter Qutb al-Din al-Husaini (Plate 133). This piece was made for a building in Kashan, and Muhammad the tailor came from Aran, a village not far distant, which suggests that the workshop responsible was situated in Kashan. Of rather different quality is the plaque recording the building of a minbar (pulpit) in the Friday Mosque of Kuhpaya (Plate 134), dated 935/1528; and different yet again is a tombstone for Mas'ud al-Shirazi dated 967/1560. This last piece is painted on an opaque white glaze, whereas the rest are on a

[4]Lane (1957, pls. 18–19) and Grube (1976, nos. 257–8).
[5]Godman (1901, pl. II, no. 359).
[6]Watson (1975b, pp.68–9, nos. 1 and 2). The frieze tiles came to light more recently, two entering the Victoria and Albert Museum in 1983. Two tiles, with inscriptions almost identical to that in the Metropolitan Museum of Art (Plate 129), differ sharply in size, material and style of execution. Discrepancies in the inscriptions suggest that they may be later copies; see Watson (1975b, no. 3), Grube (1976, no. 259) and The John Phillip Kassebaum Collection, I, Kansas, 1981, no. 13.

131 TOMBSTONE for Bibi Malik Khatun. Dated 886/1481, height 36 cm (14.1 in),
width 24 cm (9.4 in)
Musée de Sèvres, Paris, 19335. See pages 160 and 197

132 TOMBSTONE for Muhammad the tailor. Dated 891/1486, height 37.3 cm (14.7 in),
width 25 cm (9.8 in)
Art Institute of Chicago, AIC 16.145. See pages 160 and 197

133   COMMEMORATIVE TILE, in the shrine of Shah Yalman, Kashan. By QUTB AL-DIN
      AL-HUSAINI, dated 902/1496, height 43 cm (16.9 in), width 28 cm (11 in)
      In situ, *Kashan. See pages 160, 182 and 197*

134   COMMEMORATIVE TILE, in the Masjid-i Jum'a, Kuhpaya. Dated 935/1528,
      height 35 cm (13.8 in), width 26 cm (10.2 in)
      In situ, *Kuhpaya. See pages 160, 188 and 197*

crackly transparent glaze laid over a granular white frit body, with frames and borders outlined in blue. These low quality tiles represent the best endeavours of a stagnant tradition.

It is perhaps surprising to find the costly and elaborate lustre technique decorating objects of minor artistic merit. The reason may lie in the type of tile, for out of the six examples (counting pairs and the group of Abu Sa'id as single cases) three are tombstones, two record works done in religious buildings; and the remaining set—Sultan Abu Sa'id's group—may well also have been made for religious building. This religious and funerary use corresponds to that of lustre tiles in the Il-Khanid period, and perhaps this association preserved the technique, albeit in a minor way.[6a] What this meant, however, was that the technical skills required to produce the lustre were not lost, and that when fashion demanded bright and striking decoration, as it evidently did in the seventeenth century, the lustre technique was available to be exploited again; and exploited it was.

SAFAVID LUSTRE

The large number of surviving pieces attests to the revival of interest in the lustre technique in the Safavid period. It is not, however, as common as other wares of the period—in particular those painted in underglaze blue—and gives all the indications of being the product of a single workshop, or a small group of very closely related ateliers. We have no indication where these were located. Kashan, Isfahan, Kirman, Yazd and Shiraz have all been suggested, not for any very sound reasons.[7] It is tempting to see the difference in technical quality and painting skill as an indication of difference in date, though it may equally well be argued that they represent the work of different potters. We are lacking the most rudimentary documentary evidence to help us in any such division of the material.

The body is of white frit, usually compact and hard, though in pieces of lesser quality it tends to a softer and more friable material. The vessel, moulded or thrown—often in several sections—receives a coating of a white slip, possibly pure ground quartz, before the application of the transparent glaze. This latter is brilliant and close fitting on the best pieces, but tends to greenness and pooling when applied more thickly on inferior wares. The whole vessel, or parts of it, are commonly coloured a deep blue, more rarely a turquoise or lemon yellow. These colours are applied as a stain to the slip coating, which is then covered with the transparent glaze, and not, as has previously been stated, by colouring the glaze itself.[8] On a small number of

[6a]Two further tiles have come to light, one a tombstone, the other commemorating the setting up of a mihrab, see page 197, nos. 134–5.
[7]See Watson (1975a, p. 76), Lane (1957, pp. 102–4) and Pope (1939, pp, 1657–8).
[8]Lane (1957, p. 103).

135 FRAGMENT OF A TILE from a watercourse. Safavid period, length 11.2 cm (4.4 in)
Victoria and Albert Museum, C5−1913. See pages 165 and 188

pieces blue and yellow are used to paint designs under the glaze, the yellow
often outlined in black. Two systems of setting the pieces in the kiln are used.
In the better wares the whole of the base was glazed and the piece set on a
tripod leaving characteristic scars inside the footring; in other cases the foot
was wiped free of glaze and fired without a support.

The colour of the lustre pigment was generally of the same coppery tone,
but the variations from a rich metallic sheen with startling highlights of blue
and purple to a rather anaemic grey-brown would seem to be the result of
variations in the firing conditions and not of any difference in the composition
of the pigment. A deep-red colour is achieved by an overall wash of lustre on a
yellow ground; this technique is used on cups and other small pieces.

A wide variety of shapes occur: bottles, ewers, jars, bulb jars, jugs, hookah
bases, spittoons, covered pouring vessels, bowls, dishes, goblets and cups. They
are none of them very large, bottles rarely measuring more than 28 cm (11 in)
high nor dishes more than 22 cm (8.6 in) in diameter, while the majority of
articles are far smaller than this. This may well have stemmed from technical
considerations which limited the size of the lustre kiln that the potters were

then able to manage. One notable omission from their regular products is tiles—surprisingly, for tiles were the mainstay of earlier periods, and it was through tile production that the technique was preserved and communicated to the Safavid potters. Technical limitations may again have been the reason, for irregularities in the flow of the gases through the kiln have a great effect on the final appearance of the lustre. This variation would not be too noticeable on small objects, but would be all too apparent on the large plain surface of a tile. One single fragment of a tile painted in lustre and preserved in the Victoria and Albert Museum (Plate 135),[9] shows that at least on one occasion the potters took on ambitious projects. Its profile suggests that it formed part of a watercourse or fountain, and the play of light through the water on to the brilliant lustre painting must have been quite spectacular.

The shapes follow the standard repertoire of Safavid wares in general, and almost every variation can be paralleled in wares in other decorative techniques. Bottles (Plate 136, Colour Plate O), small bowls (Plate 137a, b), cups and spittoons (Colour Plate P) are common; plates (Plate 138), flower vases (Plate 139) and spouted vessels (Plate 140) are less common. A number of shapes, however, very popular amongst the blue-and-white potters, are lacking. These are closely derived from imported Chinese porcelains, and they include the deep bowl, the shouldered vase with constricted foot, the *kendi* and various dish forms. This antipathy to Chinese influence extends to the painted designs, which alone among Safavid painted wares show virtually no Far Eastern elements but are based on Middle Eastern traditions. Most commonly found are floral designs of sprays or trees, flowers and leaves growing from a low base-line. On more complicated pieces these blossom forth into a landscape populated with birds and, more rarely, with animals (Plate 138, Colour Plate O). Irises with fleshy leaves painted with a full brush are very popular, as is an unidentified plant in which something like a large poppy-head gives forth further fronds (Plate 140, Colour Plate O). Trees, spiky leaves and tufts of grasses complete the floral repertoire. Arabesques and scrollwork are used within panels and cartouches, often reminiscent of the so-called Kirman polychrome wares.[10]

It is the unique quality of these painted designs that gives the Safavid lustres their particular interest. The style of landscape and floral painting follows in spirit, though not in detail, the marginal illuminations and painted bindings of manuscripts of the previous century,[11] but neither on textiles, metalwork, ceramics nor contemporary manuscripts can one find an immediate source. We must assume it to be the individual creation of the lustre potters. Only one of these has been securely identified—a certain Khatim, whose name appears on a handful of pieces (Plate 140).[12] On a dish in Berlin-Dahlem the phrase

[9]No. C5–1913, unpublished.
[10]In Pope (1939) compare pl. 796a with pl. 801, and pl. 797e with Lane (1957, pl. 60a).
[11]Pope (1939, pls. 892–3, 896–8, 950, 974–5 etc.).
[12]Rapoport (1970).

136   BOTTLE. Dated probably 1084/1673, height 21.5 cm (8.4 in)
Present whereabouts unknown, after Wallis (1893). See pages 165, 166 and 200

amal-i Khatim (work of Khatim) in a bold calligraphic form is used as the main decorative motif against a background of floral sprays.[13] The name Muhammad Rida which is said to occur on the bottom of a bowl in the Godman Collection may be that of either potter or patron.[14]

    Only one dated piece is recorded, and its present whereabouts is unknown. The lithographed illustration given by Wallis in 1893 includes the mark on the base (Plate 136), the reading of which is by no means clear. Beneath an illegible word or phrase is written a date, read variously as 1006/1597, 1062/1651 and 1084/1673. The earliest date is most difficult to justify, and a date at some point in the second half of the seventeenth century is virtually certain. Even accepting the difference in technical quality as an indication of a difference in date, the Safavid lustres form such a homogeneous group that a very long period of production cannot plausibly be suggested, and we can do no better than agree with Arthur Lane that the wares were made largely in the second half of the seventeenth century, their decline perhaps continuing into the eighteenth century.[15]

[13]Pope (1939, p. 1658, fig. 576).
[14]London (1908, p. 21, case D, no. 15), illustrated in Godman (1901, no. 227, pl. V).
[15]Lane (1957, pp. 102–4). His brief overview remains authoritative.

137 a, b   BOWL. Safavid period, diameter 14 cm (5.5 in)
            Louvre, 3868. See page 165

138   DISH. Safavid period, diameter 21.6 cm (8.5 in)
       British Museum, 78, 12–30, 599. See page 165
139   FLOWER VASE. Safavid period, height 26 cm (10.2 in)
       Victoria and Albert Museum, 926–1876. See page 165

Although the lustre potters had the technical skill to produce other wares, they appear not to have done so in any significant quantity. A very rare type is painted in yellow and black alone, without lustre; a unique bottle of this type in the Victoria and Albert Museum is decorated with strange animals and human figures.[16] A small handful of pieces painted in blue-and-white share the same body and glaze as the lustre pieces and may have been made by the same potters, though the cutting of the footrim and other differences, particularly in the style of painting, suggest otherwise.[17]

POST-SAFAVID LUSTRE WARE

Throughout the eighteenth and early nineteenth century the lustre technique did not die out, though we have only one documented piece until a revival in the second half of the nineteenth century. A bowl in the Hetjens-Museum, Düsseldorf combines broadly painted floral motifs in a reddish lustre with rather tighter painting in underglaze blue. It is signed by Muhammad Yusuf and is dated 1212/1797 (Plate 141).[18] There are no other pieces that can be immediately related to it, though similar pieces painted in underglaze blue alone are dated in the early nineteenth century.[19]

The latter part of the nineteenth century sees yet another revival of the technique. One may suppose that it was partly due to the great interest shown by Europeans in earlier lustre wares. Major-General Sir Robert Murdoch Smith, for example, in addition to his duties as director of the Persian telegraph department, took great interest in the art and antiquities of the country. His judicious and extensive purchases, which formed the basis of the Victoria and Albert Museum's holdings of Persian art, included many lustre-painted tiles and vessels of both Il-Khanid and Safavid date. Prices paid in Europe for 'old Persian lustred ware' were very high, and important collections such as that of F. DuCane Godman were being formed. This activity coincided with experiments in the lustre technique by European art potters, William de Morgan in particular.

Murdoch Smith also interested himself in contemporary work, and in particular patronized Ali Muhammad, a young potter from Isfahan, who in 1884 moved to the capital Tehran.[20] Dated pieces by him are known from the years 1302 to 1305/1884 to 1887 (Murdoch Smith left Persia in 1888, though Ali Muhammad presumably continued to work). Ali Muhammad's production

[16]No. 978–1886.
[17]For example, three bottles in the Victoria and Albert Museum, nos. 1158–1876, 2496–1876 and 2542–1876, all unpublished.
[18]Düsseldorf (1973, no. 409). The detail photograph of the signature has become reversed with that of no. 408.
[19]For example, Hobson (1932, p. 70, fig. 86), dated 1817.
[20]Scarce (1976).

140 SPOUTED JAR. Safavid period, signed by KHATIM. Diameter 19 cm (7.5 in)
British Museum, 91, 6–17, 5. See pages 165 and 182

141 BOWL. By MUHAMMAD YUSUF, dated 1212/1797, diameter 17.1 cm (6.7 in)
Hetjens Museum, Düsseldorf, 12220. See pages 169, 182 and 200

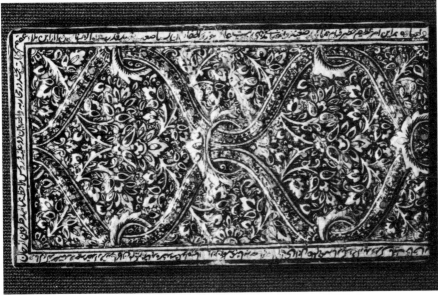

142   TILE. By ALI MUHAMMAD, made in 1887, height 20 cm (7.8 in), width
      34 cm (13.9 in)
      Victoria and Albert Museum, 567–1888. See pages 175 and 197
143   TILE. Probably by ALI MUHAMMAD, Qajar period, height 49.5 cm (19.5 in),
      width 25.5 cm (10 in)
      Hetjens Museum, Düsseldorf. See page 175

144 STAR TILE. Possibly by ALI MUHAMMAD, Qajar period, diameter 30.5 cm (12 in)
 Reitlinger Collection, Ashmolean Museum, Oxford, 1978–1579. See page 175
145 BOWL. Qajar period, diameter 16.2 cm (6.4 in)
 Victoria and Albert Museum, 1331–1904. See page 175

146   JAR. Qajar period, height 14.5 cm (5.7 in)
      Victoria and Albert Museum, 1332–1904. See page 175
147   SPITOON. Qajar period, height 12.5 cm (4.9 in)
      Victoria and Albert Museum, 1797–1909. See page 175

148 JAR. Qajar period, height 20.5 cm (8 in)
Durham University Oriental Museum, Durham, 1969–486. See page 175

consisted almost entirely of tiles, for the most part painted in a colourful polychrome. Two lustre pieces by him are known, however, and others can be attributed to him on stylistic grounds. A frieze tile in the Victoria and Albert Museum, purchased from the potter in 1887, clearly apes a thirteenth-century style, with a moulded inscription in blue against a ground of foliage reserved in white on a reddish lustre ground (Plate 142).[21] A transparent glaze is laid on a white granular body. A small mihrab, perhaps produced with more deliberate intention to deceive, or possibly designed to replace a destroyed or damaged original, bears his signature but with the date 751/1350.[22] It is of far higher quality than the frieze tile. The floral and arabesque decoration which densely covers the whole surface owes nothing to fourteenth-century design, but is typical of the florid style of nineteenth-century Persia, and can be matched on other signed and (correctly) dated pieces of Ali Muhammad's work. On the basis of these two pieces one may tentatively attribute to the same potter other large lustred plaques with moulded arabesques in a nineteenth-century style (Plate 143), and possibly a star tile (Plate 144) and jar in a rather more archaic style.[23] Ali Muhammad was asked by Murdoch Smith to write a technical description of his work, which was published in Edinburgh in 1888 under the title of *On the Manufacture of Modern Kashi Earthenware Tiles and Vases*.[24] In this detailed treatise he concentrates on the underglaze-decorated wares, and inexplicably omits all mention of the lustre technique. If his intention was to preserve a valuable secret, he was unfortunate, for lustre pieces of the late nineteenth and early twentieth centuries were produced in a style very different from his own.

A bowl and jar in the Victoria and Albert Museum (Plates 145 and 146) are both painted in the decorative and archaizing style typical of the nineteenth century. These pieces may have been made as forgeries, though they now appear distinctly of their period. More dangerous to the inexperienced eye are pieces painted in a very heavy coppery lustre, their designs and shapes being rather slovenly copies of the seventeenth-century originals (Plate 147). A number were acquired (as copies) by the Victoria and Albert Museum in 1909, and were presumably new when purchased. The vase in Plate 148 dates from some time in the first half of this century. Recent books on crafts in Persia illustrate such dismal efforts that it is evident that the technique is little understood.[25] Given the history of lustre-painted ceramics in Persia, however, it would be rash indeed to say that the technique had no future.

---

[21]Watson (1975b, pl. VIIIb) and Scarce (1976, fig. 10).
[22]Published as of fourteenth-century date by Melikian Chirvani (1966), but see Watson (1975b, pl. 77, note 28).
[23]The second plaque is in the British Museum, see Watson (1975b, pl. IXb). For the jar see Düsseldorf (1973, no. 145).
[24]Reprinted in W. J. Furnival, *Leadless Decorative Tiles, Faience and Mosaic*, Stone, 1904, pp. 215–23.
[25]J. and S. Gluck, *A Survey of Persian Handicraft*, Tehran, New York, London and Ashiya, 1977, pp. 65 and 70.

Appendix I

LUSTRE POTTERS AND THEIR WORKS

The most common form of signature on lustre wares is preceded by the word *katabahu*, literally 'wrote it', but perhaps better translated in this context as 'decorated it', for the inscriptions usually form only a very minor part of the design. The fullest phrase used is *katabahu ba'da ma 'amilahu wa sana'ahu* 'decorated after he had made and fashioned it'. *Katabahu* would therefore seem restricted to the decoration with lustre pigment, and not to prior stages which are covered by *'amila* and *sana'a*. These may refer to the different aspects of design and manufacture. In one mihrab, signed by two potters, one name is prefixed by *'amila*, the other by *sana'a*, this man also calling himself *al-katibi* 'the scribe' (pages 136 and 179). This tends to suggest that *sana'a* refers to design, leaving *'amila* to indicate the purely ceramic processes. Such technical terms are notoriously difficult to identify precisely, if indeed they were ever used in a precise fashion, and this suggestion is made with due reserve.

Some seventeen potters of the thirteenth and fourteenth centuries have been recorded, only half a dozen for the succeeding centuries. In the pre-Mongol and Il-Khanid period two families of potters are certainly known, and possibly two others. Three further potters are known by more than one work, while nine are represented by a single piece each.

The chronology of the Abu Tahir family gives an interesting, if puzzling, insight into the 'career structures' of the potters: very long gaps—twenty-eight and forty-eight years respectively—occur between the known works of the three generations, whereas one might expect the works of father and son to overlap. The 132 years between the first of Muhammad's works and the last work of his grandson, Yusuf, is a surprising length of time. By juggling the figures, one may arrive at a set of hypothetical dates which account for the period. Let us say that Muhammad was thirty when he made tiles for Qumm in 1205, and forty during his work at Mashhad in 1215. If his son Ali were born in or about that year, his first known work would have been produced at the age of twenty-seven, and his last at the age of fifty in 1265. If Ali's son Yusuf was twenty-five when he produced his first known work in 1305, his father must have been sixty-five when he was born—a good age for a medieval father. Yusuf would on this reckoning have been fifty-four when he produced his last known work in 1334. While Muhammad's recorded working life is only ten years, Ali's is twenty-five, and Yusuf's twenty-nine, both of which are less than that of Abu Zaid, with a recorded span of thirty-four working years.

THE POTTING FAMILIES

Kratschkovskaya and Pope both took delight in constructing elaborate family relationships, to account for a number of names that occur on tiles.[1] The danger is that many of these relationships are based on single names of the commonest occurrence. The Abu Tahir family is well established, for each member gives his genealogy back to Abu Tahir. The al-Husaini family is also securely identified, in that the son gives the name of both his father and grandfather. The authenticity of the al-Muqri family depends on the date and nature of the tiles which bear the putative son's name in Mashhad—and on whether the name is actually that of a craftsman rather than a patron, which is not known. Less secure is the identity of other members of the Abu Tahir family and the relations of Abu Zaid. Confusion has been caused by a frieze tile in the Godman Collection bearing the name '. . . ibn Ja'far ibn Muhammad . . .'.[2] Pope suggested Ja'far to be a brother of Abu Zaid; Kratschkovskaya proposed another son of Muhammad ibn Abi Tahir. One may suggest that the tile more probably comes from an inscription recording the names of the Shi'ite Imams, and gives those of Ja'far (al-Sadiq) and Muhammad (al-Baqir), the sixth and fifth Imams respectively. Kratschkovskaya suggests links between the Abu Tahir and al-Husaini families and of Rukn al-Din Muhammad with the latter, though only through the correspondence of the commonest of names 'Ali'. These links are implausible, if only because honorific and other parts of the names, if these connections were real, would be inexplicably inconsistent. More interesting is to note the co-operation of apparently unrelated craftsmen. The most important of these partnerships is that between Abu Zaid and Muhammad ibn Abi Tahir, who worked together at both Qumm and Mashhad. A century later Muhammad's grandson Yusuf signed a piece together with Ali of the al-Husaini family.

Abu Zaid made both tiles and vessels, and worked in both the *minai* and lustre techniques. Abu Tahir also worked in both techniques, though no tiles of his are recorded. Yusuf of the Abu Tahir family made blue and black underglaze-painted tiles in addition to his lustre tiles; no vessels by him are recorded. The remaining potters signed either vessels or tiles but (with the possible exception of Muhammad ibn Abi Tahir) not both and only in the lustre technique. This rigid specialization must be more apparent than real, and partly results from the fact that lustre tiles are more often signed than lustre vessels, and lustre ware in general is signed more often than ware in other techniques. There is, for example, no recorded signature on underglaze-painted ware of the pre-Mongol period. Taken together, the evidence points to a group of closely-knit workshops producing a variety of expensive and sophisticated wares. This is seen in the co-operation of potters as well as their work in varying techniques and types of ware. The fact that a number of potters sign their work *kataba hu* 'decorated by . . .' may indicate that they were working as decorators alone, and relied on others for the necessary ceramic skills.[3]

The bibliography on the pieces mentioned in the following list is given in the relevant places in the 'List of Dated Persian Lustre Ware' (page 189) and 'Buildings Decorated with Lustre Tiles' (page 183).

---

[1] Pope (1939, p. 1666) and Kratschkovskaya (1946, p. 17).
[2] Pope (1939, pp. 1570, 1666, pl. 725c).
[3] Ustad Jamal Naqqash ('the painter') worked in another's workshop (see above page 142) though the form of the signature which includes both *Kataba* and *'amal* suggests that he was responsible for more than just the decoration.

LUSTRE POTTERS

PRE-MONGOL AND IL-KHANID PERIODS

1. *Abu Tahir* family: a. Abu Tahir
                                       b. Muhammad ibn Abi Tahir
                                       c. Ali
                                       d. Yusuf

2. *al-Husaini* family: a. Ali ibn Ahmad ibn Ali al-Husaini
                                       b. Hasan

?3. *Abu Zaid* family: a. Abu Zaid ibn Muhammad ibn Abi Zaid
                                       b. (?brother to Abu Zaid)—Ali

?4. *al-Muqri* family: a. Muhammad ibn Abi al-Hasan al-Muqri
                                       b. Ali (potter?)

Potters with more than one work surviving:
1. al-Hasan ibn Arabshah
2. Ustad Jamal Naqqash, in the workshop of Rukn al-Din Muhammad ibn Ali

Potters with a single work surviving:
1. al-Husain ibn al-Murtada ibn Muhammad
2. Muhammad ibn Abi Mansur
3. Muhammad ibn Abi Nasr
4. Muhammad ibn Muhammad
5. Shams al-Din al-Hasani
6. Umar Ali (?)

FIFTEENTH TO NINETEENTH CENTURIES

In chronological order:
1. Diya al-Din ibn Sharaf al-Din Husain
2. Nusrat al-Din Muhammad
3. Qutb al-Din al-Husain
4. Khatim
5. Muhammad Yusuf
6. Ali Muhammad

FAMILIES

1. *Abu Tahir family*
  a. *Abu Tahir*

Two works may be suggested to be by this potter. The first is a *minai* bowl in the Museum of Islamic Art, Cairo, which is signed *Bu Tahir Husain*.[4] This may be a shortened form of the full name *Abu Tahir ibn Abi al-Husain*, which is seen in his son's signature. The second piece possibly by this potter is the monumental style bowl (page 52, Plate 16) bearing the signature '*amal (work of) Abu Tahir ibn Muhammad Hamza ibn al-Hasan. Muhammad* is here given

[4]No. 12910; see Wiet (1935a, p. 6, pl. III).

instead of the patronymic *Abu'l-Husain*. We may conceivably be dealing here with a different Abu Tahir.[5]

b. *Muhammad ibn Abi Tahir ibn Abi al-Husain*

(a) Large mihrab on tomb of Fatima in Qumm (page 124, Plate 103), undated, but other work in the tomb is dated 602/1206.

(b) Tilework in the shrine at Mashhad, dated 1215. Muhammad's signature occurs on the door surround (page 124).

(c) Central pentagonal tile from a large mihrab, undated and bearing the incomplete signature 'Muhammad . . . decorated it'.[6]

(d) Medium mihrab on the tomb of Shahzada Ahmad, Qumm. Undated and incomplete signature '. . . Tahir made it'. Probably to be attributed to Muhammad on a stylistic basis, though possibly to his son, Ali.

(e) See also Muhammad ibn Abi Nasr ibn al-Hasaini, page 181.

c. *Ali ibn Muhammad ibn Abi Tahir al-Qashani*

(a) Large mihrab in the shrine at Mashhad, dated 640/1242 (page 131, Plate 109).

(b) Fragments of a large mihrab from the Imamzada Muhammad ibn Ja'far in Gurgan (page 131).

(c) Large mihrab from the Imamzada Yahya, Veramin, dated Sha'ban 663/May 1265 (page 132).

(d) Medium mihrab from Shah Ahmad Qasim, dated Safar 663/Nov 1264 (page 185).

(e) Undated tiles on the tomb of Fatima in Qumm (page 124).

(f) Unsigned and undated large mihrab in the shrine at Najaf may be attributed to Ali by comparison with pieces (c) and (d) above (page 134).

d. *Yusuf ibn Ali Muhammad ibn Abi Tahir al-Qashani*

(a) Medium mihrab from Imamzada Yahya, Veramin, dated 10 Muharram 705/3 August 1305, and also bearing the signature of Ali ibn Ahmad of the al-Husaini family (pages 136 and 176).

(b) Frieze tile, dated Sha'ban 709/January 1310 (page 140).

(c) Frieze tile, dated Ramadan 710/January 1311 (page 140).

(d) Large mihrab from the Imamzada Ali ibn Ja'far, Qumm, dated Ramadan 734/May 1334 (page 142, Plate 120).

(e) Underglaze-painted small mihrab tile, from the Qal'a Mosque in Quhrud, dated 716, 717, 726 or 727/1316–1327.[7]

(f) Underglaze-painted frieze tile, bearing only the name . . . *ibn Muhammad al-Husaini*, but attributable to Yusuf by comparison with (e). [8]

2. *al-Husaini family*

a. *Ali ibn Ahmad ibn Ali al-Husaini*

(a) Medium mihrab, from the Imamzada Yahya in Veramin, dated 10 Muharram 705/3 August 1305, also bearing the signature of Yusuf of the Abu Tahir family (pages 136 and 176).

(b) Small mihrab of unknown provenance, one of a pair, the other being unsigned; neither is dated (page 149, Plate 125, Colour Plate N).

(c) Medium mihrab, dated 713 or 723/1313 or 1323, with incomplete signature containing only the names Ali and al-Husain(i).

---

[5]Fehérvári (1981, no. 111).
[6]Ettinghausen (1936b, fig. 25).
[7]Watson (1975a, pp. 62–3, pl. VIIIb).
[8]Sotheby's (1976a, lot 111).

b. *Hasan ibn Ali Ahmad Babuya, the builder (al-bina)*
   (a) Medium mihrab, undated, Metropolitan Museum of Art (page 142, Plate 126).[9]

3. *Abu Zaid family*
  a. *Abu Zaid ibn Muhammad ibn Abi Zaid al-Naqqash (the painter)*
   Abu Zaid has left more signed pieces than any other potter. He frequently adds the phrase *bi-khattihi* 'in his own hand' after his name, and the two words together have previously been interpreted as *Abu Zaid-i Bazi* and *Abu Rufaza*.[10]
   (a) *Minai* bowl dated 4 Muharram 583/27 March 1186 (page 70).
   (b) Fragment of a vase dated 587/1191 (page 80, Plate 53).
   (c) Dish, dated Rajab 598/March 1202.
   (d) Star tile, dated Safar 600/October 1203.
   (e) Frieze tiles in the shrine at Qumm, dated Rajab 602/February 1206 (page 124).
   (f) Dish, dated 604/1207.
   (g) Star tile, dated 607/1210 (page 127, Plate 107).
   (h) Star tile, dated Rabi' II 608/September 1211 (page 127, Plate 106).
   (i) Bowl, dated Shawwal 609/February 1213.
   (j) Star tile, dated Dhu'l-Qa'da 609/March 1213.
   (k) Star and octagonal tiles, in the shrine at Mashhad, dated Safar and Jumada 612/June and September 1215 (page 124, Plate 105).
   (l) Large mihrab in the shrine at Mashhad, dated Rabi' II 612/July 1215 (page 124, Plate 104a, b).
   (m) Bowl, dated 616/1219 (Plate 67).
   (n) Rim-sherd, undated, painted in the large-scale miniature style (pages 70 and 80).[11]
   (o) Cross tile, undated.[12]
  b. *Ali ibn Muhammad ibn Abi Zaid*
   Pope reports that this name has been read on octagonal tiles in the dado of the shrine at Mashhad and suggests him as a brother to Abu Zaid.[13] Photographs have not been published. 'Ali' is possibly a misreading for 'Abu Zaid', but were the reading substantiated the Abu Zaid family would become a certainty.

[9]Dimand (1930, p. 131, fig. 75). Dr Sheila Blair's Ph.D. Thesis on *The Shrine Complex at Natanz, Iran*, Harvard, 1981 provides some interesting information on the activities of Hasan ibn Ali. It appears (pp. 76, 127) that he signed stucco work in the shrine at Natanz and in the mosque at Mahallat-i Bala. His work at Natanz she dates to the 1320s or 1330s. This makes it unlikely that he was responsible for the lustre tilework there, dated 1307 (see p. 136), or for a stucco frieze of the same date, which she considers of too high a quality to be by him (pp. 175–6). Dr Blair suggests that the inscription on the mihrab refers to him as patron rather than potter. In view of his father's profession we may perhaps regard him as a potter who had branched into other types of building work, perhaps because of the declining demand for tiles which is apparent in this period (see p. 142). He would no doubt have had experience of working in stucco through the making of moulds necessary for the manufacture of lustre tiles. It may well be that potters with experience in this area of potting had always been also involved in stucco decoration.
[10]Bahrami (1936, pp. 183–4), Pope (1939, p. 1576), Bahrami (1946a) and Watson (in press (a)).
[11]In the British Institute of Persian Studies, Tehran. Watson (1976, pl. 12).
[12]In the Gemeente Museum, The Hague, illustrated in Watson (1977, fig. 25), otherwise unpublished. It is decorated with a half-palmette scroll containing birds, cf. Ettinghausen (1936b, fig. 2f).
[13]Pope (1939, p. 1570).

4. *al-Muqri family*
  a. *Muhammad ibn Abi al-Hasan al-Muqri*
    (a) Bowl, dated 608/1211 (page 108, Colour Plate F).
    (b) Bowl, undated, apparently decorated in both lustre and *minai* techniques. The inscription showing the signature has never been illustrated, and the present whereabouts of the bowl is unknown.[14]
  b. *Ali ibn Muhammad al-Muqri*
    This signature has been read on tilework round the door to the entrance of the tomb-chamber at the shrine in Mashhad, but is prefixed by the phrase *min 'amal* 'of the work of' which may suggest that he was a patron rather than a potter. We do not know what type of tiles these are, but should they be lustre tiles, a father–son relationship may reasonably be assumed.

POTTERS WITH MORE THAN A SINGLE SIGNED WORK SURVIVING

1. *al-Hasan ibn Arabshah al Naqqash*
  (a) Large mihrab, from the Maidan Mosque in Kashan, dated Safar 623/February 1226 (page 131).
  (b) Four tiles from a frieze are known, one of which bears the signature of al-Hasan. They are not dated (page 131).[15]

2. *Ustad Jamal Naqqash (the painter)*
  Muhammad ibn Ali
    Ustad Jamal signed two stars of a series dated in the months Rabi' I to Jumada I 738/October to December 1337 (page 142, Plate 121). The inscriptions state that the work was done '. . . in the place Kashan' in the workshop of Muhammad ibn Ali, whose full titles are given as '. . . Sayyid of Sayyids, Sayyid Rukn al-Din Muhammad son of the late Sayyid Zain al-Din Ali . . .', a third star bears the name of the workshop owner alone.

POTTERS WITH ONLY A SINGLE SIGNED WORK SURVIVING

1. *Abu Muhammad al-Husain ibn al-Murtada ibn Muhammad ibn Ahmad al-Husaini* signed a series of frieze tiles that ran round the sarcophagus of the Imamzada Ali Ja'far in Qumm. They are undated, but other tilework in the building is dated between 1305 and 1334.
2. *Muhammad ibn Abi Mansur al-Kashi* signed a bowl dated 601/1204 (page 84, note 10).
3. *Muhammad ibn Abi Nasr ibn al-Husaini* signed a small dish dated 611/1214 (page 104, Plate 74). The signature is not altogether clear and could possibly be read as Muhammad ibn Abi Tahir ibn al-Husaini, and be of the Abu Tahir family mentioned above.[16]
4. *Muhammad ibn Muhammad al-Nishapuri* signed an undated lustre bowl '. . . dwelling in Kashan' (pages 41 and 43, Colour Plate G).[17]
5. *Shams al-Din al-Hasani* signed a dish dated Jumada II 607/November 1210 (page 90, Plate 63).

[14]Pope (1936) and (1939, pp. 1597–8, pl. 705).
[15]Lane (1947, pl. 67a) and (1960, pl. 1b), Grube (1976, no. 187) and London (1908, pl. VI).
[16]Bahrami (1949a, pl. LVII). The present whereabouts of this piece is unknown.
[17]Bahrami (1949a, p. 92, pl. XLIX) and Watson (1976, p. 5) and (1979).

6. *Umar Ali* is reputed to have signed a small Il-Khanid period dish (page 111, Plate 91); the reading has been disputed.[18]

LUSTRE POTTERS OF THE FIFTEENTH TO NINETEENTH CENTURIES

1. *Diya al-Din ibn Sayyid Sharaf al-Din Husain al-Husaini* signed a lustre star, probably of fifteenth-century date (page 157, Plate 127).[19]
2. *Nusrat al-Din Muhammad* signed a building plaque for the Timurid Sultan Abu Sa'id, dated 860/1455 (page 160, Plate 129).
3. *Qutb al-Din al-Husaini* signed a plaque commemorating a donation to the shrine of Shah Yalman in Kashan, dated 902/1496 (page 160, Plate 133).
4. *Khatim*, signed a number of pieces of Safavid lustre (page 165, Plate 140).[20]
5. *Muhammad Yusuf* signed a lustre bowl, dated 1212/1797 (page 169, Plate 141).[21]
6. *Ali Muhammad*, working in Isfahan and Tehran during the last decades of the nineteenth century, made a lustred frieze tile in 1887 and signed a small mihrab falsely dated 751/1351 (page 175, Plates 142–4).[22]

[18]See above page 111, note 3 where Lane disputes the reading. Kelekian (1910, no. 48) and Pope (1939, p. 1633, pl. 722b).
[19]Watson (1975b, p. 76, pl. VII).
[20]Rapoport (1970) and Pope (1939, fig. 576).
[21]Düsseldorf (1973, no. 409). The detail photograph of the signature has become transposed with that of no. 408.
[22]Melikian Chirvani (1966), Watson (1975b, pp. 78–9, pl. VIIIb) and Scarce (1976).

Appendix II

BUILDINGS DECORATED WITH LUSTRE TILES

A good number of the tiles now in private and public collections throughout the world were collected from ruined buildings or dug up on the abandoned sites of old cities. Thus Henri d'Allemagne in 1911 recommends 'les touristes amateurs de curiosités' to go to the ruined city of Tus, where 'rien qu'en grattant le sol, on trouve les plus beaux spécimens de carraux à reflets métalliques qu'on puisse rêver'.[1] Less scrupulous means of acquisition were, however, also widely practised. Spurred on, no doubt, by the high prices paid for lustre tiles by Europeans, a band of thieves ripped the tiles from the walls of the mosque in the small town of Quhrud in about 1900. In this instance they were unsuccessful, for the inhabitants raised a hue-and-cry and pursued the desecrators of their mosque into the night. The tiles were recovered and reset, along with a finely carved door. What happened to the thieves is not recorded, but the tiles remain *in situ* to this day.[2] Similar thefts had raised the suspicions of the inhabitants of Veramin to such a pitch that when Madame Dieulafoy wished to enter the Imamzada Yahya she was confronted by a band of irate villagers wielding staves, and only the production of a letter from the Shah himself allowed her entry.[3] The villagers had every cause for concern, for a few years later the story of the shrine's despoiling is recounted by Henri d'Allemagne: a minister of the Shah Muzaffar al-Din acquired the tiles of the mihrab by an arrangement 'quelque peu louche', and smuggled them 'dissimulées parmi les bagages de son maître' to Paris, where they were eventually sold.[4] The negotiations for the removal of the mihrab from the mosque at Kashan were well drawn out. According to a catalogue of the Preece sale 'a large number of tiles comprising this mihrab were carried off surreptitiously and were secured later on, tile by tile, by Mr Preece until at length the guardian of the Masjed was induced to dispose of the remaining, and most important, portion of the panel. The negotiations to this end extended over nearly twenty years.'

Given the clandestine method by which many of the tiles came on to the antique markets of Persia, we are lucky to have as many firm indications of provenance as do survive, even though these are surely but a piteous fraction of the total. Comments on the types of buildings in which they are found are given in Chapter 11.

[1]D'Allemagne (1911, III, p. 92).
[2]Watson (1975a, p. 64).
[3]Dieulafoy (1887, p. 147).
[4]The full story can be constructed from two accounts: Godman (1903) and d'Allemagne (1911, II, p. 130).

We know of twenty-two buildings in which tiles were used. They are as follows:

Qumm: a. Shrine of Fatima
                     b. Imamzada Ja'far
                     c. Imamzada Ali ibn Ja'far
                     d. Imamzada Harith ibn Ahmad ibn Zain al-Abidin
                     e. Shah Ahmad Qasim
                     f. Shahzada Ahmad
Mashhad: Shrine of Ali Rida
Kashan: a. Masjid-i Maidan
                     b. Imamzada Habib ibn Musa
                     c. Shrine of Ali
Veramin: Imamzada Yahya
Gurgan: Imamzada Muhammad ibn Ja'far al-Sadiq
Najaf: Masjid Jami' Sar, adjoining the Shrine of Ali
Damghan: Imamzada Ja'far
Baku: Khangah Pir-i-Husain
Sarvistan: Imamzada Shaikh Yusuf Sarvistani
Quhrud: Masjid-i Ali
Natanz: Tomb of Abd al-Samad
Kharg: Imamzada Mir Muhammad Hanafiyya
Yazd: a. Buq'a Shah Kamal
                     b. Masjid-i Waqt u Sa'at
Takht-i Sulaiman: Palace of Abaqa Khan

QUMM

The town of Qumm is recorded as being a Shi'ite stronghold from as early as the tenth century. It centred round the shrine of Fatima and developed as an important religious centre. In attracted a large number of religious notables and boasts a considerable number of their tombs, many of which date from, or were decorated in, the thirteenth and fourteenth centuries.

a. *Shrine of Fatima*, sister of the eighth Shi'ite Imam Ali Rida. Probably of very early foundation, but constantly rebuilt, the lustre tiles being now the earliest remains in the shrine. The lustre tiling clads the sarcophagus, and records the names of potters Muhammad ibn Abi Tahir and Abu Zaid, with the date Rajab 602/February 1206. Later additions include work by Muhammad's son Ali. See page 124, and Tabataba'i (1976, I, pp. 46–50, pls. 2–12). Plate 103.

b. *Imamzada Ja'far*, a son of the seventh Imam Musa al-Kazim. The sarcophagus was once clad in panels of star tiles dated 665/1266. See page 134 and Tabataba'i (1976, II, pp. 38–40, pls. 11–13).

c. *Imamzada Ali ibn Ja'far.* This building contains the tombs of both Ali, son of the sixth Imam Ja'far al Sadiq, and his nephew Muhammad, son of the seventh Imam Musa al-Kazim. Lustre tiles were installed at various times: groups of star tiles dated 705 and 738 (Plate 121); a frieze by the otherwise unknown potter Abu Muhammad al-Husain ibn al-Murtada ibn Muhammad ibn Ahmad al-Husaini; another unsigned but dated Rajab 718/September 1318; a large mihrab by Yusuf ibn Ali, dated 734/1334 (Plate

120); an undated panel recording the names of the occupants of the tombs; and other friezes. The tiles are now removed to the Shrine Museum and the Tehran Museum, and their exact position in the building is not known. The frieze tiles may have clad the sarcophagus. See page 142; and Tabataba'i (1976, II, pp. 47–50, pls. 32–42), Godard (1937, pp. 309–27), Wilber (1955, no. 37).

d. *Imamzada Harith ibn Ahmad*, also known as Shahzada Ahmad, and forming part of the Khak-i Faraj complex, this building houses the tomb of Harith ibn Ahmad, grandson of Ali Zain al-Abidin, the fourth Imam. A three-tiled medium mihrab covered the top of the sarcophagus before its removal to the Tehran Museum. Tabataba'i (1976, II, pp. 83–4, pls. 138–41), Wilber (1955, no. 72).

e. *Shah Ahmad Qasim*, the tomb of the great-great-grandson of the sixth Imam Ja'far al-Sadiq. According to nineteenth-century reports, it was decorated with lustre tiles, and from one description it seems possible to identify the section of mihrab dated Safar 663/November 1264, and signed by Ali ibn Muhammad ibn Abi Tahir, formerly in the Berlin Museum, as coming from this building. Tabataba'i (1976, II, pp. 68–70, pl. 116), Ritter (1935, p. 63, taf. 2).

f. *Shahzada Ahmad*, forming part of the Shah Hamza complex, the sarcophagus of the descendant of the seventh Imam Musa al-Kazim was covered by a large three-tile panel bearing Quranic inscriptions and the incomplete signature '. . . Tahir made it'. Probably to be attributed to Muhammad ibn Abi Tahir, but possibly to his son Ali. Tabataba'i (1976, II, pp. 90–1, pls. 146–8).

MASHHAD

Shrine of Ali Rida. The tomb of the eighth Imam at Mashhad was an important shrine and pilgrimage centre at least a century before it received its decoration of lustre tiles. The tiles are still *in situ* and constitute the finest array surviving. Dado panels surmounted by friezes, a door surround and two large mihrabs were installed in 612/1215 by the potters Abu Zaid and Muhammad ibn Abi Tahir (Plates 104 and 105), and Muhammad's son Ali installed a third mihrab in 640/1242 (Plate 109). The name Ali ibn Muhammad al-Muqri is also recorded, but whether as patron or potter is unclear. The names Ali ibn Muhammad ibn Abi Zaid, Aziz ibn Adam and others have been noted, but the readings of the inscriptions have not been verified, nor have the roles of these men been ascertained. See pages 28 and 124, and Sani' al-Daula (1884, II, pp. 56–63), Donaldson (1935), Wilber (1955, no. 92), Mu'taman (1972).

KASHAN

a. *Maidan Mosque.* This mosque once contained the large mihrab by al-Hasan ibn Arabshah, dated 623/1226, now in Berlin. The mihrab cannot have been made for this structure, as the present fabric of the building is no older than the fifteenth century — a foundation inscription gives the name of the Qaraqoyunlu Sultan and the date 868/1463. The mihrab was doubtless brought from another building and installed in the fifteenth century or at a later date. See page 131 and Dieulafoy (1887, pp. 204–6), Naraghi (1970, pp. 203–37) and Lane (1947, pl. 66).[5]

---

[5]Preece (1913, no. 1); Dieulafoy saw the mihrab in situ (1887, p. 204, pl. 206); by the time Sarre visited Kashan it was gone (1910, p. 72).

b. *Imamzada Habib ibn Musa*, the tomb of a son of the seventh Imam Musa al-Kazim. The fabric of the structure has been considerably rebuilt at later dates, and only the tiles that clad the sarcophagus survive from the early decoration. A three-tile medium mihrab, dated 667–670/1268–1271 (Plate 113) originally lay on the top of the sarcophagus, three of whose sides bear frieze and star tiles (Plate 114). See page 136, Godard (1937, p. 315, pl. 138), Pope (1937, p. 155, fig. 7) and Wilber (1955, no. 14).

c. *Shrine of Ali*. A description of the building plaque has been given (page 146, Plate 124) with the unusual story of the vision of the first and twelfth Imams and the subsequent foundation of the building. Though technically not a tomb, the shrine functioned as one, and became a point of pilgrimage and the focus of a cemetery (known as the 'Place of Pilgrimage of the Foot-print of Ali') that grew up around it. It exists to this day and is situated on the north-west of Kashan, on the road out to Fin. Adle (1972) and (1982).

VERAMIN

Imamzada Yahya. Tiles were installed in this tomb-tower over a period of years. The dado contained star and cross tiles (Colour Plate K) dated 1262, a large mihrab by Ali ibn Muhammad dated 663/1264, and a medium mihrab which may well have once covered the sarcophagus and is signed by two potters and dated 705/1305. See page 132. Wilber (1955, no. 11) and Pope (1939, pl. 400).

GURGAN (modern Gunbad-i Qabus)

Imamzada Muhammad ibn Ja'far. In the basement of this largely modern building were found fragments of a large mihrab signed by Ali ibn Muhammad. The present tomb, that of a son of the sixth Imam Ja'far al-Sadiq, is on the site of an old one, recorded as far back as the fourteenth century, and in all probability dating back to the period of the mihrab or earlier. See page 43 and Bahrami (1949a, p. 75).

NAJAF

Masjid Jami' Sar. In a mosque that adjoins the tomb-chamber of Ali ibn Abi Talib, the first Imam, are reset sections of a large mihrab that can be attributed to Ali ibn Muhammad. Najaf was noted as an important shrine by the tenth century, and has remained so to the present day. See page 134, and Aga Oglu (1935).

DAMGHAN

Imamzada Ja'far. A series of stars and crosses dated 665/1267 (Plate 110) were found in the entrance chamber to this tomb of a distant descendant of the fourth Imam, Ali Zain al-Abidin. Their 'secular' motifs led to suggestions that the tiles were the re-used decoration of an unidentified palace (see pages 134 and 154). Sani' al-Daula (1884, II, pp. 272–4), Wilber (1955, no. 13), Bahrami (1936 and 1939).

BAKU

Khangah Pir-i Husain. This khangah, or Sufi hostel, is centred on the tomb of a Sufi shaikh, whose tomb-chamber was extensively decorated with lustre tiles. Frieze tiles and stars covered the walls and the sides of the sarcophagus, while a coffin-like construction of tiles capped the sarcophagus. Dates range from 1282 to 1285. There is no direct Shi'ite connection with this building, though the shaikh's name, Husain ibn Ali, suggests sympathy with the Shi'ite Imams. See page 136 and Kratschkovskaya (1946).

SARVISTAN

Imamzada Shaikh Yusuf Sarvistani. A structure, now ruined, that contained the tombs of this Sufi shaikh, and two others, bearing dates of 680/1281, 710/1310, 714/1314 and others. Lustre tiles were seen here at the end of the last century, but have since been removed and are not identified. Shaikh Yusuf's religious affiliation is not known, though other names in the tomb, as at Baku, suggest a sympathy with the Shi'ite Imams. Dieulafoy (1887, pp. 211–12), Wilber (1955, no. 20).

QUHRUD

Mosque of Ali. This mosque was founded after a vision of the first Imam appeared to Abd al-Wahid ibn Muhammad, a local religious leader, an event which is recorded in an inscription on the carved wooden door. Two batches of stars were installed: the first of the same date as the door, 700/1300, the second in 707/1307 (Plate 115). A plaque dated 736/1335 is installed in the mihrab. They were reset at the beginning of this century and we do not know what position they first occupied. The earlier tiles are inscribed with Quranic quotations, the later with Persian verse. See pages 136 and 155, Watson (1975a).

NATANZ

Tomb of Abd al-Samad. In 707/1308 this tomb-chamber was extensively decorated with lustre tiles as part of an ambitious building plan that extended the mosque and added a khangah. Dado panels of frieze tiles (Plate 116) and stars covered the walls, and an elaborate three-dimensional mihrab or tombstone was constructed (Plate 117). These have all since been removed. The star tiles have not been positively identified. Shaikh Abd al-Samad's adherence to the Shi'ite sect is demonstrated by the occurrence of the phrase 'Ali is the Friend of Allah' on the façade of the building. See pages 136 and 154, Wilber (1955, no. 39).

KHARG

Imamzada Mir Muhammad Hanafiyya is the tomb of a son of the first Imam Ali ibn Abi Talib. It has dados of lustre stars some of which are still *in situ*, dated 738/1337. All are inscribed in Persian verse. See page 142, Wilber (1955, no. 102), Al-i Ahmad (1975, pp. 80–5).

YAZD

In the course of restoration work fragments of tiles have been found in three buildings, two of which are complexes of tomb-chambers: *Buq'a Shah Kamal* and *Masjid-i Waqt u Sa'at*. Quantities of stars and a few fragments of frieze tile were found but none in any original position. We may assume that they came from the tomb-chambers. A madrasa—Masjid-i Shah Abu 'l-Qasim—contains a single star that may be re-used. All three buildings date from the first half of the fourteenth century. See Wilber (1955, nos. 67, 113), Afshar (1976, I, pp. 604–7, 610–13 and 562–70).

Palace of Abaqa Khan. This building was decorated with lustre stars and both figural and epigraphic frieze tiles. The tiles are dated between 670 and 674/1271–5, but none survive *in situ*. This is the sole domestic building of the period to have been excavated. (Plate 112 and Colour Plate La). See pages 134 and 156, and Naumann (1976).

These buildings are the only ones we can identify for certain as having originally had lustre decoration. Tiles have been found a number of times in the ruins of cities. Thus at Qutchan and Tus, Henri d'Allemagne towards the end of the last century talks of finding lustre tiles,[6] and more have turned up at Qutchan.[7] Aurel Stein picked up fragments of tiles at Shahr-i Ij, and at Gah, where they were found on the site of a large cemetery.[8] Wilber, upon finding fragments of tiles in the ruins of the Ghazaniyya—the suburb founded by Sultan Ghazan on the outskirts of Tabriz—suggested they came from Ghazan's mausoleum which was situated there.[9] Fragments of Kashan stars and of later types have been picked up among ruins on the Qal'a Ardeshir and the Qal'a Dukhtar in the town of Kirman.[10] At Marv, Russian excavations have revealed some tiles *in situ* in a section of a building called a 'citadel' whose function is not entirely clear.[11] Slightly different are the single tiles re-used, probably at quite recent date, in two mosques at 'Aqada and Bidakhawid in the Yazd area'.[12]

The tiles found in the Gunbad-i Shaikh Shu'ibi at Khonj are probably also re-used and their evidence for dating the building to the Il-Khanid period is doubtful; half-tiles are set in narrow friezes on the exterior.[13] We must also regard with some suspicion the report of the lustre half-tile coming from the mausoleum of Pir-i Bakran at Linjan, for there is no other lustre decoration in the building.[14] Several 'mihrab' tiles show by their inscriptions that they are tombstones, and must have originally come from tomb-chambers: the tombstone of Khadija, daughter of the sixth Imam, Ja'far al-Sadiq, dated 713 or 723/1313 or 1323; the tombstone of Husain Zain al-Abidin, the fourth Imam;[15] the tombstone of an unidentified Qadi[16] and a tombstone of a person whose name appears on a missing section, dated 688/1289.

The handful of tiles that occur after the Il-Khanid period are again mostly funerary (pages 157–63). Three are tombstones—for Bibi Malik Khatum, for Muhammad the tailor and for Mas'ud Shirazi—while another records a donation to the tomb of Shah Yalman in Kashan. The nature of Abu Sa'id's building mentioned in the texts on his lustre tiles is not known, while the tile in Kuhpaya is the only certain instance of a lustre tile used to record building work in a mosque which has no funerary or commemorative function.[17] Dated 935/1528, it is almost two centuries later than the last of the main run of Kashan lustre tilework (Plate 134). The sole Safavid tile, almost two hundred years later in date again, has all the appearance of being purely secular (Plate 135).

[6]D'Allemagne (1911, II, p. 122; III, p. 92).
[7]Shakiri (1968, p. 172).
[8]Stein (1936, pl. XXVII) and (1937, pp. 98–9).
[9]Wilber (1955, no. 27).
[10]Watson (1975b, p. 75).
[11]Gyuzalyan (1949, pp. 418-19).
[12]Afshar (1970, pp. 37 and 360–70).
[13]Gropp (1970, p. 189).
[14]Bahrami (1938, p. 259) and Wilber (1955, p. 121).
[15]Murdoch Smith (n.d., pp. 32–3) and Cust and Fry (1913).
[16]Wallis (1894, pl. X) and Godman (1903, p. 25, fig. X). This piece from the Godman Collection is now in the British Museum.
[17]See page 163, note 6a.

Appendix III

LIST OF DATED PERSIAN LUSTRE WARE

The following is a list of dated pieces, based on that by Ettinghausen in the *Survey of Persian Art*,[1] and it includes pieces discovered since that time, both published and unpublished. One significant point has been established since he wrote—the form of the figure '5'. In lustre ware of the period under consideration both circle and dot are used for zero, though the circle has at times been read as '5', as in the modern o or ◌. On lustre tiles '5' is always written ☉, and the circle always indicates zero.[2] Thus the numeral dating of stars begins as early as 607 (nos. 4 and 5 below), not in 631 as Ettinghausen suggests,[3] while the earliest vessel dated in numerals is the dish of 598/1202. An asterisk (*) after the list number indicates that the piece appeared in Ettinghausen's list, and where there is no source other than a mention in Ettinghausen's list, his number is quoted in the form (E. no. 000). Further references will be found where appropriate in the lists of potters and buildings (pages 176 and 183).

DATED PERSIAN LUSTRE TILES

1.* 600, Safar/October 1203. Star, with four figures. Arab Museum, Cairo, no. 3162. Wiet (1933, p. 32, no. 30, pl. XIX).

2. 602, Rajab/February 1206. Frieze by *Abu Zaid* on the tomb of Fatima, in Qumm. Tabataba'i (1976, I, pl. 9).

3.* 604, Sha'ban/February 1208. Star, with two figures. Museum of Fine Arts, Boston, no. 11.40. Ettinghausen (1936a, I, p. 148, fig. 2). Plate 108.

4.* 607/1210. Star, with two figures. Museum of Fine Arts, Boston, no. 07.670. Signed by *Abu Zaid*. Bahrami (1936, pl. LXVc). Plate 107.

---

[1]Ettinghausen (1939).
[2]The reading of the circle had caused problems to Kühnel, Bahrami and Ettinghausen, see Bahrami (1936, pp. 181 and 184–5), Ettinghausen (1939, p. 1677, no. 44, note 4). The problem is resolved by a study of the stars at Quhrud, where ٧٥٥, ٧٥٠ and ٧٠٠ all occur frequently, along with the date in words 'seven hundred'. Watson (1975a, pp. 73–4) gathers all pieces dated in numerals which contain zero or five, and it is seen that five always occurs in the form ☉, and that both • and ○ stand for zero.
[3]Ettinghausen (1939, p. 1670).

5.* 607/1210. Fragment of star, with epic scene? Islamic Museum, East Berlin, no. I
487. Bahrami (1936, p. 184, pl. LXVIb).

6. 608, Rabiʻ II/September 1211. Star, with horseman. Museum of Fine Arts,
Boston, no. 07-903. Signed by *Abu Zaid*. Ettinghausen (1936a, I, pp. 145–6,
fig. 1).[4] Plate 106.

7.* 608, Rajab/December 1211. Star, with two seated figures. Pennsylvania
Museum of Art, Philadelphia. Bahrami (1937, p. 54, fig. 20).

8.*5 608/1211. Star, with seated figure. Arab Museum, Cairo. Wiet (1933, p. 35,
no. 34, pl. XXII).

9.* 609, Dhuʼl-Qaʻda/March 1213. Star, with figure in landscape. Arab Museum,
Cairo. Signed by *Abu Zaid*. Wiet (1935a, p. 5, no. 9, pl. II).

10.* 610/1213. Fragment of cross. Kunstgewerbe Museum, Leipzig. (E. no. 33).

11. 612/1215. During this year the shrine of Ali al-Rida in Mashhad was extensively
decorated with lustre tiles. A door surround, signed by *Muhammad ibn Abi
Tahir* is dated Jumada I; a large mihrab by *Abu Zaid* is dated Rabiʻ II; star and
octagonal tiles in the dado, some signed by *Abu Zaid*, are dated Safar and
Jumada I, and a frieze that bears the date 512 is a copy of a century later. The
tiles are still *in situ*. Saniʻ al-Daula (1884, II, pp. 56–63), Donaldson (1935),
Muʻtaman (1972). Plates 104 and 105.

12.* 613, Dhuʼl-Qaʻda/February 1217. Octagonal tile, with three figures. Islamic
Museum, East Berlin, no. 1529. Bahrami (1937, p. 58), Grube (1961, fig. 7).

13.* 614, Dhuʼl-Hijja/March 1218 (possibly =714/1314). Star, with hares in
geometric design. Present whereabouts unknown. London (1885, no. 147),[6]
Wallis (1894, fig. 14).

14.* 616/1219. Half-star, with two figures. Metropolitan Museum of Art, New
York, no. 66.95.5. Pope (1939, p. 1578).

15.* 616, Jumada II/August 1219. Panel of two stars and cross, with arabesque
designs. Pennsylvania Museum of Art, Philadelphia, no. 16.167. Elkins (1934,
p. 86, fig. 3).[7]

16. 617, Dhuʼl-Hijja/February 1221. Star, in very poor condition. Ex-Bahrami
Collection. Bahrami (1946b, fig. 12).

17.* 623, Safar/February 1226. Large mihrab, from the Masjid-i Maidan in Kashan.
Islamic Museum, East Berlin. Signed by *al-Hasan ibn Arabshah*. Kühnel
(1928, pp. 126–35), Lane (1947, pl. 66).

18.* 624, Safar/January 1227. Star, with figure riding a camel. Art Museum of the
Ukrainian Academy of Science, Kiev. Gyuzalyan (1956).

19.* 626, Jumada I/April 1229. Star, with arabesque design. Walters Art Gallery,
Baltimore, no. 48. 1289. Ettinghausen (1936a, I, pp. 148–9, fig. 3).

20.* 627, Rabiʻ II/February 1230. Star, with arabesque design. (E. no. 41).

21.* 627, Shaʻban/June 1230. Half-star, with arabesque design. Ex-Herzfeld
Collection. (E. no. 41a).

22.* 631/1233. Fragment of star tile. Ettinghausen Collection. (E. no. 42).

---

[4]Ettinghausen (1936a, II, pp. 227–8) withdrew a reading of 603 for this tile, on the grounds that
a break and restoration obscured the units of the date. Grube (1961, fig. 6) publishes a
photograph of the tile after the restoration had been removed, and the date 608 can be clearly
read, as Bahrami had already suggested (1937, p. 54, fig. 19).
[5]No date can be seen on any of the photographs of a tile said by Ettinghausen to be dated
608/1211 (E. no. 29).
[6]Ettinghausen erroneously attributes this tile to the Godman Collection (1939, no. 36).
[7]Ettinghausen (1939, no. 34) dates this tile 610.

23. 640/1242. Large mihrab by *Ali ibn Muhammad ibn Abi Tahir*, in the shrine of Ali al-Rida in Mashhad. Sani' al-Daula (1884, p. 62), Donaldson (1935, p. 127), Plate 109.

24.* 653, Ramadan/October 1255. Tile from a medium mihrab. Ex-Preece Collection. Preece (1913, no. 9, pl. 1).

25. 654/1256. Star, with three figures. Private collection, Tehran. Bahrami (1949b, p. 119, no. 108). Possibly a misreading for 604/1207.

26. 656, Jumada II/June 1258. Cross with animal-headed scrolls. Collection unknown. Godard (1937, pp. 328–9, fig. 148).

27.* 660–661/October to December 1262. In the three months Dhu'l-Hijja 660 to Safar 661 were made a large number of star and cross tiles that decorated the dado of the Imamzada Yahya in Veramin. All are decorated with geometrical, floral or arabesque designs. Over 150 examples are recorded in some twenty-four collections. Bahrami (1937, pp. 87–91) and London (1976, no. 379). Colour Plate K.

28.* 661/1262. Star, with three horsemen. Shrine Museum, Qumm. Pope (1937, fig. 5), Godard (1937, fig. 147).

29.* 663, Sha'ban/May 1265. Large mihrab, from the Imamzada Yahya in Veramin. Ex-Kevorkian Collection, now in a private collection in the United States. Signed by *Ali ibn Muhammad ibn Abi Tahir*. Pope (1939, pl. 400).

30.* 663, Safar/November 1264. Medium mihrab, said to be from Qumm, possibly from the tomb of Shah Ahmad Qasim. Islamic Museum, East Berlin, said to have been destroyed during the war. Signed by *Ali ibn Muhammad ibn Abi Tahir*. Kühnel (1931, fig. 13).

31* 663, Ramadan/June 1265. A group of some thirty stars was made in this month. Their provenance is unknown, but their designs closely resemble those of the Veramin group (above no. 27), although they are smaller in size. The Metropolitan Museum of Fine Arts, New York, contains about half the surviving examples, the remainder are in various other collections. Grube (1962, fig. 3), Bahrami (1937, fig. 41).

32.* 664–5/September 1266 to April 1267. In the months Dhu'l-Hijja 664 to Ramadan 665 a number of tiles were made, which have traditionally been attributed to the Imamzada Ja'far in Damghan. A number of tiles which had been seen and described *in situ* are now mounted in a panel in the Louvre, Paris, no. 3619. Other pieces are preserved in various collections. Bahrami (1936, pp. 186–9), (1937, pp. 93–111) and (1939). Plate 110.

33. 665/1266. A small group of tiles, from the Imamzada Ja'far, Qumm, united by a characteristic form of foliage, were made in this year. The dated tile is in the Gulbenkian Museum of Oriental Art, Durham, no. 1971–52, the remainder are split between various collections. Watson (1983).

34.* 665/1266. Tile from a medium mihrab. Victoria and Albert Museum, London, no. 469–1888. Wallis (1894, fig. 39), Pope (1945, pl. 81). Plate 111.

35.* 665/1266. Star, fragmentary. Two seated figures drinking, with reserved inscription. Kelekian Collection. (E. no. 59).

36. 666, Dhu'l-Qa'da/July 1268. Star, with two seated figures, lustre very faint. Islamic Museum, West Berlin, no. I 30/68a. Berlin (1971, no. 478).

37. 667–670/1268, August 1271 and September 1271. A medium mihrab in the Iran Bastan Museum, Tehran, no. 3289, is dated with three different dates: 667, Muharram 670 and Safar 670. It once lay on the tomb of the Imamzada Habib ibn Musa in Kashan. Godard (1937, p. 317, fig. 138). Plate 113.

38. 667, Jumada I/January 1269. Star, with two seated figures. Fogg Museum, Harvard University. Binghampton (1975, no. 40).

39.* 667/1268. Star, with an animal in foliage. Collection H. Naus Bey, Cairo. Wiet (1935b, no. C51) and (1935c, pl. 30a).

40.* 668/1269. Small mihrab. Victoria and Albert Museum, no. 1519–1876. Watson (1977, p. 144, fig. 179).

41.* 668/1269. Small mihrab, from the same mould as no. 40. Ex-Dillon Collection. London (1885, no. 148).

42. 668, Rabi‘ I/November 1269. Star, with two seated figures. Art Institute of Chicago, no. 39.381. Day (1941, p. 55, fig. 1).

43.* 669/1270. Star, with flower motif. Kunstindustrimuseet, Oslo. (E. no. 64).

44. 669/1270. Fragment of star, found in the ruins of old Qutchan. Shakiri (1968, p. 172).

45.* 66–/1261–1270. Two frieze tiles, one dated 66–. Ex-Porcher-Labreuil Collection. (E. no. 48). Porcher-Labreuil (1934, no. 145, and pl. VII).[8]

46. 670–674/1271–1275. The summer palace of the Mongol Abaqa Khan was decorated during this period with lustre tiles of different varieties. Star tiles alone were dated, with dates of 670, 671 and 674. Stars included examples with reserved border inscriptions, and two types with painted inscriptions. Lustre frieze tiles found with them must also be assumed to have been made during these years. Naumann (1976). Plate 112, Colour Plate La.

47.* 670, Dhu'l-Hijja/July 1272. Star, with gazelle. Iran Bastan Museum, Tehran, no. 3949. Unpublished.

48. 672/1273. Star, with two figures. Present whereabouts unknown. Made with a flat base and only seven points. Bahrami (1946b, fig. 13), Barcelona (1950, no. 100).

49.* 672/1273. Star. Iran Bastan Museum, Tehran. (E. no. 66).

50. 673/1274. Star, with three seated figures. Gerald Reitlinger Collection, Ashmolean Museum, Oxford.

51. 673/1274. Star, with running antelope. Present whereabouts unknown. Bahrami (1946b, fig. 14).

52.* 675/1276. Small mihrab. Walters Art Gallery, Baltimore, no. 48.1310. Ettinghausen (1936a, I, pp. 149–50, fig. 4).

53. 676 or 677/1277–8. Star, with floral design and hare. Iran Bastan Museum, Tehran, no. 3565. Unpublished.

54.* 678/1279. Star, with floral design and two dogs. Louvre, Paris. Bahrami (1937, p. 111, fig. 14).

55. 678/1279. Star, with two seated figures. Royal Ontario Museum, Toronto, no. 961.167. Heinrich (1963, p. 25, no. 3).

56.* 678/1279. Star, with lion. Kelekian Collection. Exhibition of P. Cassirer, Berlin, 1911, no. 177. (E. no. 69).

57.* 679, Rabi‘ II/August 1280. Star, with plant motif. Hermitage Museum, Leningrad. Kratschkovskaya (1946, pl. XXII/2).

58.* 679/1280. Star, with two figures. Ex-Filippo Collection. Filippo Sale, American Art Galleries, December 1918, no. 446. (E. no. 70).

59.* 679/1280. Star, with floral motifs. Present whereabouts unknown. Wiet (1935a, p. 8, note 1).

60. 680/1281. Star, with arabesque design and reserved inscription. Victoria and Albert Museum, London, no. 509c–1888.

61.* 680 or 681/1281 or 1282. Star, with nursing camel; reserved inscription. Ettinghausen Collection. Ettinghausen (1936a, II, pp. 224–5, fig. 7).

[8]I have been unable to trace this publication.

62. 680/1281. Star, with gazelle. Iran Bastan Museum, Tehran, no. 3520. Godard (1936, p. 181, fig. 125).

63. 680, Jumada I/August 1281. Star, geometric design, with birds. Ciccio Collection, Capodimonte. Naples (1967–8, no. 51, fig. 39).

64. 680/1281. Star, with arabesque design. Present whereabouts unknown. Sotheby's (1976a, no. 200).

65. 680/1281. Star, fragmentary and restored, with floral and arabesque motifs. Kashan Museum, Fin, Kashan. Unpublished.

66. 681, Safar/May 1282. Star, with arabesque and bird designs. Islamic Museum, West Berlin. Berlin (1971, no. 479).

67.* 681–684/1282–1285. Star tiles made in these four years were used to decorate the tomb of Pir-i Husain in Baku. They bear geometrical, floral and animal designs. A frieze dated 684 records the renovation of the building and the names and titles of Pir-i Husain. A complex structure of tiles, including stars, frieze tiles and specially shaped pieces was used to clad the structure of the sarcophagus. Why the span of dates is so wide is inexplicable, as the tiles all appear to have been installed at the same time. The tiles are now in Leningrad. Kratschkovskaya (1946).

68.* 682/1283. Star, with floral design and two hares; reserved inscription. Kelekian Collection. Kühnel (1931, p. 228, fig. 12).

69.* 682/1283. Star, with figure in building; reserved inscription. National Museum, Stockholm. Kühnel (1924, fig. 5), Bahrami (1937, fig. 52).

70. 682/1283. Star, with floral arabesque motifs. Present whereabouts unknown (on market in Tehran in 1971). Unpublished.

71. 682/1283. Star, with tree and addorsed animals. Pope Collection, Shiraz. Unpublished.

72.* 685/1286. Star, with floral design. Victoria and Albert Museum, London, no. 29–1899. Evans (1920, pl. II/5), Watson (1975a, p. 74, fig. 4, no. 7).

73.* 686/1287. Star, with running cow. Museum of Fine Arts, Boston, no. 11.2803. Ettinghausen (1936a, II, p. 222, fig. 5).

74. 687/1288. Star, geometric design with birds. Islamic Museum, West Berlin, no. I 3/71. Berlin (1971, no. 480).

75. 687/1288. Star, floral design with two hares. Present owner unknown. Sotheby's (1976a, no. 105).

76. 687/1288. Star, design with birds. Present owner unknown. Sotheby's (1976a, no. 106).

77.* 688, Jumada II/June 1289. Lower tile of medium mihrab. Louvre, Paris, no. 3342. Bernus-Taylor (1982, p. 224, fig. 81).

78.* 688/1289. Star, floral design with birds. Islamic Museum, Berlin. Bahrami (1937, fig. 51).[9]

79.* 688/1289. Star, floral design with running fox. Arab Museum, Cairo, ex-Kazarouni Bey Collection. Wiet (1935b, p. 27, no. C52), (1935c, pl. 30).

80.* 688/1289. Star, floral design with two birds. Ettinghausen Collection, at the Baltimore Museum of Art, L.58.8.66. Grube (1962, fig. 11).

81.* 688/1289. Star, with flying birds. Present whereabouts unknown, from Ahmad of Paris. (E. no. 86).

82.* 689, Rabi' II/April 1290. Small mihrab. Collection Ibrahim Beyham, Beirut. Formerly in the Higgins Collection, London. London (1885, no. 150), Beirut (1974, no. 77).

[9]This is presumably one of the stars referred to by Ettinghausen (1939, no. 83), who appears to be quoting Kühnel (1931, p. 228). The Godman star he refers to is not dated.

83.   689, Dhu'l-Qa'da/November 1290. Star, with arabesque design. Islamic Museum, West Berlin, no. I 9/55. Berlin (1971, no. 481).

84.* 689/1290. Star, with two seated figures. Kelekian Collection, New York. (E. no. 88).

85.   689/1290. Star with enthroned figure and attendants. Gerald Reitlinger Collection, Ashmolean Museum, Oxford. Inscription in reserve.

86.* 689/1290. Star. (E. no. 89). The source quoted—Hormoz Mirza (1914)—contains no dated tile.

87.   689/1290. Two stars with zebra and horse respectively. David Collection, Copenhagen. 12 & 13—1963.

88.   691/1291. Star, with two seated figures. Private collection, London.

89.   691/1291. Two stars. National Museum of Oriental Art, Rome. Naples (1967–8, no. 53. In note).

90.* 696, Jumada II/April 1297. Star, with arabesque design. Louvre, Paris. Bahrami (1937, p. 115, fig. 53).

91.* 697/1297. Star, with arabesque design. Cassirer Collection, Berlin. Kühnel (1931, p. 228, fig. 11—interchanged with star dated 682, no. 68 above).

92.* 698/1298. Star, with main design of inscription, and reserved inscription border. Isfahan Museum. Said to have been found in the Imamzada Pir-i Bakran, Linjan (page 188). Bahrami (1938, p. 257, fig. 1), Bahrami (1949b, p. 123, no. 161).

93.   700, Rabi' I/November 1300. A batch of some 250 tiles, 65 dated, was installed in this year in the Masjid-i Ali in Quhrud. The designs show a variety of floral and arabesque motifs. They remain *in situ*. One tile of the series, dated 700, is preserved in the Victoria and Albert Museum, London, no. 561–1900 (E. no. 93). Watson (1975a, pp. 63–5, pls. I–III), see no. 102 below. Plate 115.

94.* 701/1301. Star, with arabesque design. Iran Bastan Museum, Tehran. (E. no. 94).

95.   701/1301. Star, with floral decoration. Victoria and Albert Museum, London, no. 734b–1888. Watson (1975a, p. 74, no. 9). This tile dates a group of some thirteen tiles, all preserved in the Victoria and Albert Museum.

96.* 702, Rabi' II/November 1302. Star, fragmentary with seated figure. Ex-Porcher–Labreuil Collection. Porcher–Labreuil (1934, no. 141, pl. VII).

97.* 704, Dhu'l-Qa'da/May 1305. Star, with floral design. Khawam Collection. Wiet (1935a, p. 36, no. C122).

98.* 705, 10 Muharram/3 August 1305. Medium mihrab. Hermitage Museum, Leningrad. Tombstone from the Imamzada Yahya in Veramin. Signed by *Ali ibn Ahmad ibn Ali al-Husaini* and *Yusuf ibn Ali (ibn) Muhammad*. Ritter (1935, pl. 4).

99.   705, Muharram/July 1305. Star, floral design with rabbit. Iran Bastan Museum, Tehran. Godard (1937, p. 324, fig. 145). This tile is closely related to a group dated 710, see below no. 110. They are said to be from the Imamzada Ali ibn Ja'far in Qumm.

100.* 705/1305. Star, with kneeling camel. Museum of Fine Arts, Boston, no. 31.730. Inscription in reserve. Ettinghausen (1936a, II, p. 226, fig. 8).

101.* 707/1307. Tile from a medium mihrab. Victoria and Albert Museum, London, no. 71–1885. From the shrine at Natanz. Ettinghausen (1935, pp. 58–9, fig. 18); Lane (1960, p. 5, pl. 4a). Plate 117. See no. 103.

102. 707, Rabi' II/October 1307. Sixty stars, twenty bearing this date, were installed in the Masjid-i Ali in Quhrud. They are close in design to those of 700 in the same building, see no. 93. Watson (1975a).

103.* 707, Shawwal/March 1308. Frieze tile, from the shrine at Natanz, with cornice decoration including birds. Metropolitan Museum of Art, New York, no. 12.44. Dimand (1928–9, p. 101, fig. 3). Some twenty tiles from this frieze survive in various collections. Watson (1977, p. 99). Plate 116.

104.* 707, Dhu'l-Hijja/June 1308. Small mihrab. Victoria and Albert Museum, London, no. 1483–1876. Murdoch Smith (n.d., p. 32).

105.* 707/1307. Star, with arabesque design. Ex-Harding Smith Collection, London. Wallis (1894, fig. 23). This tile is possibly identical with the following piece.

106.* 707/1307. Star, with arabesque design. Kunstindustrimuseet, Copenhagen. (E no. 99).

107.* 709, Sha'ban/January 1310. Frieze tile. British Museum, London, no 78, 12.30, 574. Hobson (1932, p. 97, fig. 114), Ettinghausen (1936b, p. 53, fig. 14). One other tile from the same series bears the signature of *Yusuf ibn Ali ibn Muhammad ibn Abi Tahir*, see Bahrami (1936, pl. LXIV). Seven more tiles from the same series in various collections are known.

108.*[10] 710/1310. Medium mihrab. Collection of the Calouste Gulbenkian Foundation, Lisbon. Ex-Arthur Collection. Kühnel (1924, fig. 6) and Gulbenkian (1963, no. 27).

109.* 710, Ramadan/January 1311. Frieze tile. Arab Museum, Cairo, no. 3746. Ettinghausen (1936b, p. 53, figs. 12–13). A tile in the Kevorkian Collection, New York, bears the signature of *Yusuf ibn Ali ibn Muhammad ibn Abi Tahir*, see Pope (1939, pl. 725e). No further pieces are known.

110. 710/1310. Star, floral decoration, with two running gazelles and two rabbits. Iran Bastan Museum, Tehran, no. 3874. Unpublished. This tile forms part of a group that includes the tile dated 705, no. 99, some of which are said to be from the Imamzada Ali ibn Ja'far in Qumm, see Godard (1937, p. 324, fig. 145).

111.* 710/1310. Star, with spotted horse and reserved inscription. Museum of Fine Arts, Boston, no. 31.729. Ettinghausen (1936a, II, p. 226, fig. 9). Plate 119.

112. 711/1311. Star, with floral decoration. Pope Collection, Shiraz. Unpublished.

113. 711, 1 Shawwal/9 February 1312. Plaque recording a vision of Ali, the first Imam. From the shrine of Ali, Kashan. Adle (1972) and (1982). Plate 124.

114. 713 or 723, Rabi' II/July 1313 or April 1323. Medium mihrab. Kevorkian Collection, New York. Tombstone for Khadija ibn Ja'far, signed by *Ali . . . al-Husaini*.

115. 713/1313. Frieze re-used in large mihrab dated 734, below no. 123. Godard (1937, p. 317, fig. 141). Plate 120.

116. 713/1313. Star. A star in the Ettinghausen Collection is restored from fragments, one of which includes the date 713. The main fragment is from a star of a series dated 738, below no. 127. Ettinghausen (1936b, fig. 19).

117. 717/1317. Star, with floral decoration. Iran Bastan Museum, Tehran. (E. no. 109).

118. 718/1318. Frieze, possibly from the Imamzada Ali ibn Ja'far in Qumm. Shrine Museum, Qumm. Tabataba'i (1976, p. 50, fig. 39).

119. 720/1320. Star with two parrots. Fogg Museum, Harvard, 1940.343. Unpublished.

---

[10]Ettinghausen (1939, no. 103) actually refers to no. 103 above, dated 707. The mistake can be traced back through Kühnel (1931) to Murdoch Smith (n.d., p. 32), where the date is misquoted.

120.   721, Jumada I/June 1321. Star, with design of two figures fighting. Iran Bastan Museum, Tehran, no. 3518. Said to come from the Imamzada Ali ibn Ja'far in Qumm. Godard (1937, pp. 326–7, fig. 146a).

121.   723, Jumada II/June 1323. Star, with deer in foliage. Metropolitan Museum of Art, New York. Unpublished.

122.*   729, Shawwal/August 1329. Star, with moulded floral decoration. British Museum, London, no. 1907, 6.10, 2. Hobson (1932, p. 97, fig. 116), Pope (1939, pl. 723c).

123.*[11] 734, Ramadan/May 1334. Large mihrab. Iran Bastan Museum, Tehran, no. 3270. From the Imamzada Ali ibn Ja'far in Qumm; signed by *Yusuf ibn Ali ibn Muhammad ibn Abi Tahir*. Godard (1937, pp. 316–17, figs. 139–43). Two frieze tiles missing from the mihrab are in the Metropolitan Museum, New York, no. 40.181.6. See Grube (1962, figs. 17–18). Plate 120.

124.   738, Dhu'l-Hijja/June 1338. Frieze tiles. Victoria and Albert Museum, London, nos. 1490 to e-1876, Royal Scottish Museum, Edinburgh, no. 1921/1317, and the Musée des Arts Décoratifs, Paris. Ettinghausen (1935, p. 60, fig. 19).

125.   738, Muharram/July 1337. This date can be read on a star from a group still *in situ* in the Imamzada Muhammad al-Hanafiyya on the island of Kharg. Decorations with inscriptions and animal designs are recorded. Only one piece is known to have been removed from the monument, and is now in the Ashmolean Museum in Oxford, see Preece (1913, no. 34, pl. 2). Al-i Ahmad (1975, p. 85) gives the most detailed information available.

126.*   738, Rabi' I to Jumada I/October to December 1337. A group of thirty-eight stars are known, of which thirteen are dated within these months. The majority are preserved in the Shrine Museum in Qumm, but some are found in other collections. The tiles are said to have come from the Imamzada Ali ibn Ja'far in Qumm. Three tiles bear the name of the owner of the potting workshop; two include the name of the potter: the workshop of *Sayyid Rukn al-Din Muhammad ibn Ali*, and the potter *Ustad Jamal Naqqash*. Pope (1937, pp. 156–61, fig. 8); Godard (1936, p. 369, fig. 237). Plate 121.

127.*   738, Rabi' I to Jumada II/October 1337 to January 1338. A group of eleven stars bear dates within these months, and several are inscribed with the phrase '. . . in Kashan'. The tiles are preserved in various collections, and the most detailed publication is by Ettinghausen (1936b, pp. 59–61, figs. 16–20).

128.*   739/1338. Star, with two figures. British Museum, London, no. OA + 1123. Related to the group no. 127 above. Hobson (1932, p. 98, fig. 117), and London (1976, no. 383). Inscribed 'in Kashan'. Plate 122.

129.*   739, Safar/August 1338. Star, with throne scene. Islamic Museum, Berlin. Related to group no. 127 above. Kühnel (1931, fig. 10, date misread as 669).

130.*   739, Safar/August 1338. Star, with inscription in main field. E. Guérin Collection. (E. no. 132).

131.   739, Dhu'l-Hijja/June 1339. Star, with design of hare. Iran Bastan Museum, Tehran, no. 3883. Inscribed 'In Kashan'. Related to group no. 127 above. Unpublished.

132.*   740/1339. Star, with floral design. Formerly Preece Collection. Related to group no. 127 above. Wallis (1894, pl. 23), Preece (1913, no. 37, pl. 2).

---

[11]Ettinghausen (1939, no. 111), a tile from Kharg in the Preece Collection, is not dated but belongs to a group dated 738, see no. 124.

133.*   860/1455. Pair of tiles, recording the erection of a building by Sultan Abu Sa'id. Metropolitan Museum of Art, 30.95.26; and Islamic Museum, East Berlin, I. 3940. Watson (1975b, pp. 68–9). Plate 129.

134.   883, Rajab/October 1478. Tombstone for Ala al-Din Fathallah', width 20.3 cm (8 in). Sotheby's, *Islamic Works of Art*, 18 April 1984, lot 158.

135.   886/1481. Tile recording the building of a mihrab, now in the Masjid-i Panj'ali in Qumm. Tabataba'i (1976, II, p. 122).

136.   886/1481. Tombstone for Bibi Malik Khatun. Musée de Sèvres, 19335. Watson (1975b, p. 70). Plate 131.

137.*   891/1486. Pair of tombstones for Muhammad the tailor. Art Institute of Chicago, 16.145; and Museum of Islamic Art, Cairo, 8170. Watson (1975b, pp. 71–2), Grube (1974, figs. 69–70). Plate 132.

138.   902/1496. Tile, recording a pious donation. *In situ* in the tomb of Shah Yalman, Kashan. Signed by *Qutb al-Din al-Husaini*. Watson (1975b, pp. 72–3). Plate 133.

139.   914/1508. Tombstone. Museum of Islamic Art, Cairo, 23482.

140.   935, Muharram/September 1528. Tile recording the donation of a minbar to a mosque. *In situ*, Masjid-i Jum'a, Kuhpaya. Watson (1975b, pp. 73–4). Plate 134.

141.*   967, Jumada II/January 1560. Tombstone for Mas'ud of Shiraz. Museum für Kunst und Gewerbe, Hamburg. Watson (1975b, p. 74).

142.   Mihrab tile, falsely dated 751/1351, signed by the late nineteenth-century potter *Ustad Ali Muhammad*. Present whereabouts unknown. Melikian-Chirvani (1966), Watson (1975b, p. 77). See page 175.

143.   Inscription tile, by *Ustad Ali Muhammad*. Not dated but purchased as new in Tehran in 1887. Victoria and Albert Museum, 567–1888. Watson (1975b, p. 77). Plate 142.

DATED PERSIAN LUSTRE VESSELS

1.*   575, Muharram/June 1179. Jar. British Museum, London, 1920, 2–26, 1. Pope (1939, pl. 636b), Hobson (1932, fig. 25) and Gyuzalyan (1966). Plate 37.

2.*   587, Safar/March 1191. Bowl. Art Institute of Chicago, 1927/414. Kühnel (1931, figs. 2–3), Pope (1939, pl. 638). Plate 38.

3.   587/1191. Fragment of a vase. Ex-Bahrami Collection. Signed by *Abu Zaid*. Bahrami (1949a, pl. 96) and Watson (1976, pl. 106). Plate 53.

4.   590, Jumada I/May 1193. Dish. Khalili Collection. Fehérvári (1981, no. 112), Plate 39.

5.   595/1198. Bottle. Islamic Museum, West Berlin, no. 1. 46/70. Berlin (1971, no. 414). Plate 54.

6.   595, Dhu'l-Hijja/September 1199. Rim-sherd of dish. British Institute of Persian Studies, Tehran. Watson (1976, pl. 11). Plate 55.

7.   598, Rajab/March 1202. Dish. Private collection, Tehran. Bahrami (1946a, pl. 16a) and (1946b, figs. 1–2).

8.*   600/1203. Bowl. Kevorkian Collection. Ettinghausen (1936b, fig. 9).

9.*   600, Jumada II/February 1204. Bowl. Kelekian Collection. (E. no. 4).

10.   601, Safar/September 1204. Bowl. Iran Bastan Museum, Tehran, no. 4395. Bahrami (1949a, pl. VIb).

11.   603, Jumada I/November 1206. Goblet. Foroughi Collection, Tehran. Unpublished.

12.   604, Muharram/July 1207. Bowl. Tillinger Collection, Tehran. Bahrami (1949a, p. 128, pl. LXIV).

13.   604, Jumada II/December 1207. Bowl, fragmentary. Iran Bastan Museum, Tehran. Unregistered and unpublished. The name 'Ahmad' appears on the base.

14.*   604/1207. Lobed dish. Ashmolean Museum, Oxford, Reitlinger Collection. Signed by *Abu Zaid*. Watson (1975a, p. 74, no. 4).[12]

15.*   604/1207. Lobed dish. Victoria and Albert Museum, C51–1952. Pope (1939, pl. 703b). Colour Plate E.

16.*   606, Rabi' I/September 1209. Bowl. British Museum, Hobson (1932, figs. 45–45a).

17.*   607, Jumada II/November 1210. Bowl. Havermayer Collection, Metropolitan Museum of Art, New York, 41.119.1. Pope (1939, pl. 709). Plate 66.

18.*   607, Jumada II/November 1210. Dish. Freer Gallery, Washington, 41.11. Signed by *Shams al-Din al-Hasani*. Pope (1939, pl. 708), Ettinghausen (1961). Plate 63.

19.   607, Jumada II/November 1210. Bowl. Metropolitan Museum of Art, New York, 61.40. Grube (1965, pl. 28).

20.   607, Ramadan/February 1211. Bowl. H. K. Monif Collection.

21.   607, Shawwal/March 1211. Bowl. Tillinger Collection. Bahrami (1949a, p. 129, pl. LXI).

22.   607/1210. Bowl. Tillinger Collection. Bahrami (1949a, p. 129, pl. LIV).

23.   607/1210. Bowl. Iran Bastan Museum, Tehran, 3179. Unpublished.

24.   607/1210. Bottle. Kufar Collection, Tehran. Bahrami (1949b, p. 111, no. 12).

25.*   608, Safar/July 1211. Dish. University Museum, Philadelphia, NE-P 19. Pope (1939, pl. 710), Kühnel (1931, fig. 5). Plate 64.

26.   608, Shawwal/March 1212. Bowl. Ex-Kelekian Collection. Christie's (1976, lot 110). The date is partially missing, leaving only 'in the year eight . . .'.

27.   608/1211. Bowl. Iran Bastan Museum, Tehran, 8224. Signed by *Muhammad ibn Abi al-Hasan*. Rome (1956, no. 374). Colour Plate F.

28.   608/1211. Bowl. Ashmolean Museum, Oxford, 1956.33. Allan (1971, pl. 28), Fehérvári (1973, no. 105).

29.   609/1212. Ewer. Boston Museum of Fine Arts, 57.150. Unpublished.

30.   609/1212. Bowl. Okayama Municipal Museum of Oriental Art. Tokyo (1982, I–47).

31.*   609, Muharram/June 1212. Bowl. Walters Art Gallery, Baltimore. Ettinghausen (1936a, figs. 8 and 29).

32.   609, Shawwal/February 1213. Bowl. Bahrami Collection. Signed by *Abu Zaid*. Bahrami (1946a, pls. 17b and 18a).

33.   609, Shawwal/February 1213. Bowl. Freer Gallery of Art, 81.29.

34.   610/1213. Bowl. Iran Bastan Museum, Tehran. Unregistered and unpublished.

35.   611, Jumada II/October 1214. Bowl. Whereabouts unknown. Bahrami (1949a, pp. 129–30).

36.   611, Shawwal/February 1215. Saucer on three feet. Etchecopar Collection. Bahrami (1949a, p. 130, pl. LVII). Plate 74.

37.   611, Dhu'l-Hijja/April 1215. Sherds of a dish. Iran Bastan Museum, Tehran. Unregistered and unpublished.

38.   611, Dhu'l-Hijja/April 1215. Bowl. Private collection, Tehran. Bahrami (1946b, fig. 9).

[12]Ettinghausen (1939, no. 16) reads the date of this piece as 654, mistaking the circle for a five rather than a zero.

39.   612/1215. Bowl. Godard Collection, Tehran. Godard (1937, fig. 152).

40.   613/December 1216, January 1217, March 1217. Several fragmentary vessels dated in various months of the year 613 have been recorded. Pieces with the months Ramadan and Shawwal are illustrated by Bahrami (1949a, p. 103, fig. 22, and p. 105, fig 23). Further pieces with these months and one with the month Dhu'l-Hijja are preserved in an unregistered sherd collection in the Iran Bastan Museum, Tehran.

41.   614/1217. Bowl. Clement Ades Gift to Victoria and Albert Museum, C160-1977. Watson (1979, fig. 4). Plate 70.

42.   614/1217. Bowl. Private Collection, Osaka, Japan. Tokyo (1982, I-20).

43.   614, Muharram/April 1217. Bowl. Matossian Collection. Bahrami (1949a, p. 131, pl. LII).

44.   614, Safar/May 1217. Dish. Possession D. Kelekian, 1950 (photo in Victoria and Albert Museum archives).

45.   614, Jumada I/August 1217. Bowl. Museum für Islamische Kunst, Berlin, I.3/56. Berlin (1971, no. 353).

46.   614, Jumada II/September 1217. Bowl. Matossian Collection. Bahrami (1949a, pp. 93-4, pl. LXXIII).

47.   614, Jumada II/September 1217. Bowl. Possession Yazdani, London, 1982. Unpublished.

48.   614, Jumada II/September 1217. Bowl. Private collection, Kanagawa prefecture, Japan. Tokyo (1982, I-33).

49.   614/March 1218, May 1217, September 1217. Fragments of four vessels dated Dhu'l-Hijja 614 are preserved in an unregistered sherd collection in the Iran Bastan Museum, Tehran. Photographs of two bowls, one dated Jumada II 614, the other Safar 614, are preserved in the photographic archives of the Ceramics Department of the Victoria and Albert Museum.

50.   614, Shawwal/January 1218. Bowl, al-Sabah Collection, Kuwait. Jenkins (1983, p. 54). Plate 71.

51.   615/1218. Bowl. Museum für Islamische Kunst, Berlin, I 2307. Kühnel (1924, fig. 2).

52.* 615/1218. Bowl. Victoria and Albert Museum, C1233-1919. Watson (1976, pl. 8).[13] Plate 87.

53.   615/1218. Bowl. Walters Art Gallery, Baltimore, 48.1242. Unpublished.

54.   615, Muharram/March 1218. Two sherds from an unregistered sherd collection in the Iran Bastan Museum, Tehran.

55.   616, Shawwal/December 1219. Rim-sherd of a bowl preserved in an unregistered sherd collection in the Iran Bastan Museum in Tehran.

56.* 616/1219. Bowl signed by *Abu Zaid*. Gemeentemuseum, The Hague, OC(1) 55-1932. Pope (1939, pls. 707a-b), London (1976, no. 350). Plate 67.

57.   616/1219. Lobed dish. Iran Bastan Museum, Tehran. Godard (1937, pp. 330-2, fig. 150).

58.   616/1219. Box. Metropolitan Museum of Art, 66.95.5. Grube (1965, p. 225).

59.   617/1220. Bottle. Private collection, Tehran. Bahrami (1946b, fig. 7).

60.* 619/1222. Bowl. Kelekian Collection. (E. no. 14a).

61.   621/1224. Rim-sherd of a bowl. Musée de Sèvres, Paris. Unpublished.

62.* 624/1226. Bowl. Kelekian Collection. Pope (1939, pl. 773b).

[13]Date read as 619 by Ettinghausen (1939, no. 14).

63.*   659/1260. Bowl. Rabenou Collection. (E. no. 17).[14]

64.   660/1261. Dish. Private collection, Gifu prefecture, Japan. Tokyo (1982, I–44).

65.   667/1268. Dish. David Collection, Copenhagen, Isl. 96. Leth (1975, p. 48). Plate 89a, b.

66.*   668/1269. Bowl. Kelekian Collection. Pope (1939, pl. 774a).

67.*   669/1270. Bottle. Godman Collection. Pope (1939, pl. 718b), Gyuzalyan (1951, pp. 43–5, pls. 5–6).

68.   670/1271. Bowl. Royal Scottish Museum, Edinburgh, 1971/687. Unpublished.

69.*   672/1273. Bowl. Hermitage Museum, Leningrad. (E. no. 20).

70.*   673/1274. Bowl. Ex-Kalebjian Bros. (E. no. 21).

71.*   674/1275. Ewer. Taylor Collection. London (1908, no. C.15, pl. XI).

72.*   676/1277. Dish. Freer Gallery of Art, Washington, 09.317. Ettinghausen (1936a, pp. 222–4, fig. 6), Washington (1973, no. 74).

73.*   681/1282. Fragment of bowl. Musée des Arts Décoratifs, Paris. (E. no. 24).

74.*   683/1284. Dish. Walters Art Gallery, Baltimore, 48/1033. Kelekian (1909, fig. 13).

75.   822/1418. Bowl. Present whereabouts unknown. Sold in Paris (1981, lot 70). See page 157.

76.*   1006/1597, 1062/1651 or 1084/1673. Bottle with trees on a blue glaze. The second or third suggestions are more plausible than the first. Present whereabouts unknown. Watson (1975b, p. 76). Plate 136.

77.   1212/1797. Bowl, signed by *Muhammad Yusuf*. Hetjens Museum, Düsseldorf, 12220. Düsseldorf (1973, no. 409, p. 272), detail of signature and date interchanged with no. 408. Plate 141.

---

[14]Ettinghausen (1939, no. 17) does not state whether this piece is dated in numerals. If it is so dated, it might well be another example of a circle being misread as five instead of zero. The piece may be dated 609.

BIBLIOGRAPHY

The Harvard system of bibliography is used here. Works are listed by author according to date of publication. References in footnotes consist of the author's name, followed, in brackets, by the date of a particular publication, together with the relevant page or illustration numbers. Occasionally works of minor relevance to the subject, which are only referred to once, are given in full in the footnotes and are not included in the bibliography.

Where a full reference is not given in the main body of the text, it will often be found either in Appendix II 'Buildings Decorated with Lustre Tiles' or in Appendix III 'List of Dated Persian Lustre Ware'. These two appendices, together with Appendix I 'Lustre Potters and their Works', comprise the documentary foundations of the study.

Ades, R. (1949)   'Persian Pottery . . . at Gurgan', *Illustrated London News*, ccxv, 3 December

Adle, C. (1972)   'Un disque de fondation en céramique (Kashan, 711/1312)', *Journal Asiatique*

Adle, C. (1982)   'Un Diptyque de Fondation en Céramique lustrée (Kashan, 711/ 1312)', *Art et Société dans le Monde Arabe*, ed. C. Adle, Bibliothèque iranienne, no. 26

Afshar, I. (1967) (ed.)   *Arayis al-Jawahir wa Nafayis al-Atayib* by Abu'l-Qasim Abd-Allah Kashani, Tehran

Afshar, I. (1970)   *Yadgarha-yi Yazd*, I, Tehran

Afshar, I. (1976)   *Yadgarha-yi Yazd*, II, Tehran

Aga Oglu, M. (1935)   'Fragments of a Thirteenth Century Mihrab at Nedjef', *Ars Islamica*, II

Al-i Ahmad, J. (1975)   *Jazira-yi Kharg*, Tehran

Allan, J. W. (1971)   *Mediaeval Middle Eastern Pottery*, Oxford

Allan, J. W. (1973)   'Abu'l-Qasim's Treatise on Ceramics', *Iran*, XI

Allan, J. W. (1974)   'Some Observations on the Origins of the Medieval Persian Faience Body', *Colloquy no. 4*, Percival David Foundation, University of London, held 25–28 June 1973

d'Allemagne, H. R. (1911)   *Du Khorassan au Pays des Backhtiaris*, 4 vols., Paris

Anon (1947)   'Gurgan Potteries recently excavated at Gunbad-i Kabuz', *Illustrated London News*, ccxi, 27 September

Bahrami, M. (1936)   'Le problème des ateliers d'étoiles de faïence lustrée', *Revue des Arts Asiatiques*, X

Bahrami, M. (1937)   *Recherches sur les Carreaux de Revêtement Lustré dans la Céramique Persane du XIIIᵉ au XVᵉ siècles*, Paris

Bahrami, M. (1938)   'Some Examples of Il-Khanid Art', *Bulletin of the American Institute for Iranian Art and Archaeology*, V/3

Bahrami, M. (1939)   'La reconstruction des carreaux de Damghan d'après leurs inscriptions', *IIIᵉ Congrès International d'Art et d'Archéologie Iraniens* (1935), Moscow

Bahrami, M. (1946a)   'A Master Potter of Kashan', *Transactions of the Oriental Ceramic Society*, 1944–5

Bahrami, M. (1946b)   'Further Dated Examples of Persian Ceramic Wares', *Bulletin of the Iranian Institute*, VI

Bahrami, M. (1947a)   'Contribution à l'étude de la céramique musulman en Iran', *Athar-e Iran*, III

Bahrami, M. (1947b)   'Faiences Emaillées et Lustrées de Gurgan', *Artibus Asiae*, X

Bahrami, M. (1949a)   *Gurgan Faiences*, Cairo

Bahrami, M. (1949b)   *Sanaʻ-yi Iran, Zuruf-i Sufalin*, Tehran

Barcelona (1950)   *Doscientos Piezas de Ceramica Persa*, Catalogo de la Exposicion, Palacio de la Viveina

Beirut (1974)   *Art Islamique dans les collections privées Libanaises*, Musée Nicolas Sursock, 31 May to 15 July

Berlin (1971)   *Museum für Islamische Kunst, Katalog*, Berlin-Dahlem

Bernus-Taylor, M. and Moulierac, J. (1982)   'Plaques Il-Xanides au Musée du Louvre', *Art et Société dans le Monde Iranien*, Paris

Binghampton (1975)   *Islam and the Mediaeval West*, Loan exhibition at the University Art Gallery, State University of New York

Caiger-Smith, A. (1973)   *Tin-Glaze Pottery*, London

Caiger-Smith, A. (1985)   *Lustre Pottery: Technique, Tradition and Innovation in Islam and the Western World*, London

Christie's (1976)   *Fine Persian and Islamic Works of Art*, 15 November, London

Combe, E. et al (1913–1964)   *Répertoire Chronologique d'Epigraphie Arabe*, vols. 1–16, Cairo

Cust, L. and Fry, R. (1913)   'Two Persian Lustred Panels', *Burlington Magazine*, XXIII

Day, F. E. (1941)   'A Review of "The Ceramic Art in Islamic Times"', *Ars Islamica*, VIII

Dayton, J. and Bowles, J. (1977)   'Abu'l-Qasim of Kashan and the Problems of Persian Glazing', *Annali dell' Istituto Orientale di Napoli*, 37

Dieulafoy, J. (1887)   *La Perse, la Chaldée et la Susiane*, Paris

Dimand, M. S. (1928–9)   'Dated Specimens of Mohammedan Art', *Metropolitan Museum of Art Studies*, I, New York

Dimand, M. S. (1930)   *A Handbook of Mohammedan Decorative Arts*, New York

Donaldson, D. M. (1935)   'Significant Mihrabs in the Haram at Mashhad', *Ars Islamica*, II

Düsseldorf (1973)   *Islamische Keramik*, exhibition held at the Hetjens-Museum

Elkins, E. C. (1934)   'Two Dated Persian Tiles', *The Pennsylvania Museum Bulletin*, XXIX

Erdmann, K. (1935)   'An Open Question in Islamic Ceramics', *Bulletin of the American Institute for Persian Art and Archaeology*, IV/2

Ettinghausen, R. (1935)   'Important Pieces of Persian Pottery in London Collections', *Ars Islamica*, II

Ettinghausen, R. (1936a) 'Dated Persian Ceramics in Some American Museums', *Bulletin of the American Institute for Persian Art and Archaeology*, part I in IV/3, part II in IV/4

Ettinghausen, R. (1936b) 'Evidence for the Identification of Kashan Pottery', *Ars Islamica*, III

Ettinghausen, R. (1939) 'Dated Faience', in Pope (1939)

Ettinghausen, R. (1961) 'The Iconography of a Kashan Lustre Plate', *Ars Orientalis*, IV

Ettinghausen, R. (1970) 'The Flowering of Seljuk Art', *Journal of the Metropolitan Museum*, 3

Evans, M. M. (1920) *Lustre Pottery*, London

Fehérvári, G. (1973) *Islamic Pottery, a Comprehensive Study based on the Barlow Collection*, London

Fehérvári, G. and Safadi, Y. (1981) *1400 Years of Islamic Art*, Khalili Gallery, London

Godard, Y. A. (1936) 'Étoiles à huit rais en faïence lustrée', *Athar-e Iran*, I/1

Godard, Y. A. (1937) 'Pièces datées de céramique de Kashan à décor lustré', *Athar-e Iran*, II/2

Godman, F. D. (1901) *The Godman Collection of Oriental and Spanish Pottery and Glass*, London

Godman, F. D. (1903) 'Lustre Ware and the Godman Collection', *Connoisseur*, VII

Gropp, G. (1970) 'Bericht über eine Reise in West- und Südiran', *Archaeologische Mitteilungen aus Iran*, 3

Grube, E. (1961) 'Some Lustre Tiles from Kashan in American Collections', *Pantheon*, XIX

Grube, E. (1962) 'Some Lustre Painted Tiles from Kashan', *Oriental Art*, VIII

Grube, E. (1965) 'The Art of Islamic Pottery', *Bulletin of the Metropolitan Museum of Art*, February

Grube, E. (1966) 'Islamic Sculpture: Ceramic Figurines', *Oriental Art*, N.S. XII

Grube, E. (1974) 'Notes on the Decorative Arts of the Timurid Period', *Gurura-jamanjarika: Studi in Honore di Giuseppe Tucci*, Naples

Grube, E. (1976) *Islamic Pottery of the Eighth to the Fifteenth Century in the Keir Collection*, London

Gulbenkian (1963) *Oriental Islamic Art, Collection of the Calouste Gulbenkian Foundation*, Museu Nacional de Arte Antiga, Lisbon

Gyuzalyan, L. T. (1949) 'Frieze Tiles of the 13th century with Poetic Fragments', *Epigrafika Vostoka*, III (in Russian)

Gyuzalyan, L. T. (1951) 'A Fragment of the Shahnama on Ceramics of the 13th-14th centuries', *Epigrafika Vostoka*, part I in IV, part II in V (in Russian)

Gyuzalyan, L. T. (1953) 'Two excerpts from Nizami on Tiles of the 13th and 14th centuries', *Epigrafika Vostoka*, VII (in Russian)

Gyuzalyan, L. T. (1956) 'Inscription on a Lustre Tile of 624/1227 in the Kiev Museum', *Epigrafika Vostoka*, XI (in Russian)

Gyuzalyan, L. T. (1961) 'A Few Poetical Texts on Veramin Tiles in the Hermitage', *Epigrafika Vostoka*, XIV (in Russian)

Gyuzalyan, L. T. (1966) 'An Inscription on a Lustre Jar of 1179 from the British Museum', *Epigrafika Vostoka*, XVII (in Russian)

Gyuzalyan, L. T. and Dyakanov, M. M. (1949) 'Notes on Star Tiles of the XIIIth century from the Village of Novaya-Nisa', *Trudy Yuzhno-Turkmenistanskoi Arkheologicheskoi Kompleksnoi Ekspeditii*, I, Ashkabad (in Russian)

Heinrich, T. A. (1963) *Art Treasures in the Royal Ontario Museum*, Toronto

Hobson, R. L. (1932)   *A Guide to the Islamic Pottery of the Near East*, London
Jenkins, M. (1983)   *Islamic Art in the Kuwait National Museum; the Al-Sabah Collection*, London
Kelekian, D. K. (1909)   *The Potteries of Persia*, Paris
Kelekian, D. K. (1910)   *The Kelekian Collection of Persian and Analogous Potteries*, Paris
Kiani, Y. (1974)   'Recent Excavations in Gurgan', *The Art of Iran and Anatolia*, Percival David Foundation Colloquy no. 4, University of London
Kratschkovskaya, V. A. (1946)   *Les Faïences du Mausolée du Pir-Houssein*, Tbilissi (in Russian, with French résumé)
Kühnel, E. (1924)   'Datierte Persische Fayencen', *Jahrbuch der Asiatischen Kunst*, I
Kühnel, E. (1928)   'Zwei Persische Gebetnischen aus Lüstrierten Fliesen', *Berichte aus den Preussischen Kunstsammlungen*, XLIX
Kühnel, E. (1931)   'Dated Persian Lustred Pottery', *Eastern Art*, III
Lane, A. (1947)   *Early Islamic Pottery*, London
Lane, A. (1957)   *Later Islamic Pottery*, London
Lane, A. (1960)   *A Guide to the Collection of Tiles*, Victoria and Albert Museum, London
Leth, A. (1975)   *The David Collection, Islamic Art*, Copenhagen
London (1885)   *Illustrated Catalogue of Persian and Arab Art*, Burlington Fine Arts Club
London (1908)   *Exhibition of the Faience of Persia and the Nearer East*, Burlington Fine Arts Club
London (1976)   *The Arts of Islam*, The Arts Council of Great Britain, Hayward Gallery
London (1979)   *Exhibition of Islamic Art: Iranian Lustreware of the Thirteenth Century*, Mansour Gallery
Melikian Chirvani, S. (1966)   'The Sufi Strain in the Art of Kashan', *Oriental Art*, XII
Melikian Chirvani, S. (1967)   'Trois Manuscrits de l'Iran Seldjoukide', *Arts Asiatiques*, XVI
Murdoch Smith, R. (*c.* 1876)   *Persian Art*, South Kensington Museum Art Handbooks, London
Mustafa, M. (1961)   *The Museum of Islamic Art, A Short Guide*, Cairo
Mustaufi, (1958)   *Nuzhat al-Qulub*, ed. M. Siyaqi, Tehran
Mu'taman, A. (1972)   *Rahnama-yi Tarikhi-yi Astana-yi Quds-i Radawi*, Mashhad
Naples (1967–8)   *Arte Islamica a Napoli*, Opere delle Raccolte Pubbliche Napoletane
Naraghi, A. (1970)   *Athar-i-Tarikhi-yi Shahristanha-yi Kashan Wa Natanz*, Tehran.
Naumann, R. (1976)   *Takht-i Suleiman*, Ausstellunskataloge der Prähistorischen Staatssammlung, Munich
Paris (1971)   *Arts de l'Islam*, exhibition held at the Orangerie des Tuileries
Paris (1981)   *Art Musulman*, sale at Nouveau Drouot, 14 April
Piccolpasso, C. (1980)   *I tre Libri dell'Arte del Vasaio*, introduction by R. Lightbown and A. Caiger-Smith, London
Pope, A. U. (1936)   'A Signed Kashan Mina'i Bowl', *Burlington Magazine*, LXIX
Pope, A. U. (1937)   'New Findings in Persian Ceramics of the Islamic Period', *Bulletin of the American Institute for Iranian Art and Archaeology*, V/2
Pope, A. U. (1939)   *A Survey of Persian Art*, 6 vols., Oxford
Pope, A. U. (1945)   *Masterpieces of Persian Art*, New York
Porcher-Labreuil (1934)   *Catalogue des Faïences Orientales et Européenes*, Galerie Labreuil, Nice, 19–21 March

Preece, J. R. (1913)   *The Collection formed by J. R. Preece at the Vincent Robinson Galleries*, London

Rapoport, I. (1970)   'Objects of Late Iranian Ceramics signed by the Master Hatim', *Soobschcheniya Gosudarstvennogo Ermitazha*, 31 (in Russian)

Ritter, H., Rusaka, J., Sarre, F., and Winderlich, R. (1935)   'Orientalische Steinbücher und Persische Fayencetechnik', *Istanbuler Mitteilungen*, III

Rome (1956)   *Mostra d'Arte Iranica*, Istituto Italiano per il Medio ed Estremo Oriente, July–August

Sani' al-Daula, M. H. K. (1884)   *Matla' al-Shams*, 3 vols., Tehran

Sarre, F. (1910)   *Denkmäler Persischer Baukunst*, Berlin

Scarce, J. (1976)   'Ali Mohammad Isfahani, Tile maker of Tehran', *Oriental Art*, N.S. XXII/3

Schmidt, E. F. (1936)   'Rayy Research . . . 1935, Part I', *University Museum Bulletin, Philadelphia*, VI

Shakiri, R. A. (1968)   *Jughrafiyya Tarikhi-yi Quchan*, Mashhad

Sotheby's (1976a)   *Islamic Ceramics, Metalwork, Arms and Armour, Glass and other Islamic Works of Art*, London, 12 April

Sotheby's (1976b)   *Islamic Works of Art, Part II*, London, 22 November

Stein, A. (1936)   'An Archaeological Tour in the Ancient Persis', *Iraq*, III/2

Stein, A. (1937)   *Archaeological Reconnaissances in North-Western India and South Eastern Iran*, London

Stern, S. M. and Walzer, S. (1963)   'A Lustre Plate of Unusual Shape with the Name of the Owner', *Oriental Art*, 9

Tabataba'i, M. (1976)   *Turbat-i Pakan*, Qumm, 2 vols.

Tokyo (1982)   *Exhibition of Lustre Ware*, organized by Asahi Newspaper Co., exhibited at the Takashima Department Store

Wallis, H. (1891)   *The Godman Collection, The Thirteenth Century Lustred Vases*, London

Wallis, H. (1893)   *Typical Examples of Persian and Oriental Art*, I, London

Wallis, H. (1894)   *The Godman Collection, The Thirteenth Century Lustred Wall-Tiles*, London

Washington (1973)   *Ceramics from the World of Islam*, Freer Gallery of Art

Watson, O. (1975a)   'The Masjid-i Ali, Quhrud: an Architectural and Epigraphic Survey', *Iran*, XIII

Watson, O. (1975b)   'Persian Lustre Ware, from the 14th to the 19th Centuries', *Le Monde Iranien et l'Islam*, III

Watson, O. (1976)   'Persian Lustre-Painted Pottery; the Rayy and Kashan Styles', *Transactions of the Oriental Ceramic Society*, XL

Watson, O. (1977)   *Persian Lustre Tiles*, Ph.D. Thesis, University of London, unpublished

Watson, O. (1979)   'Persian Wares: the Clement Ades Gift to the Victoria and Albert Museum', *Connoisseur*, January

Watson, O. (1981)   'A Syrian Bull', *Apollo*, January

Watson, O. (1983)   'Two Persian Tiles', *Arts of Asia*, 13/vi

Watson, O. (in press (a))   'Documentary *Minai* and Abu Zaid's Bowls', to be published in the proceedings of the Edinburgh University Symposium on Seljuk Art, 1982

Wiet, G. (1933)   *L'Exposition Persane de 1931*, Musée Arabe du Caire, Cairo

Wiet, G. (1935a)   'L'Epigraphie Arabe de l'Exposition d'Art Persan du Caire', *Mémoires de l'Institut d'Egypte*, XXVI

Wiet, G. (1935b)   *L'Exposition d'Art Persan*, Cairo

Wiet, G. (1935c) *Album de l'Exposition d'Art Persan*, Cairo

Wilber, D. N. (1955) *The Architecture of Islamic Iran, the Il-Khanid Period*, Princeton

Wolfe, L. (1975) *The Lester Wolfe Collection of Persian Pottery and Metalwork*, Sotheby, Parke Bernet, New York, 14 March

Yaqut (1866–73) *Mu'jam al-Buldan*, ed. F. Wüstenfeld, Leipzig

Zander, K. (1914) Sale Catalogue of the Zander Collection, Müller and Company, Paris, 14 May

Index